Copyright

Copyright © 2020 by Sophie & Chris Brousseau
All rights reserved.

No part of this book may be reproduced or transmitted in any form or by any means, electronic or mechanical, including photocopying, recording, or by any information storage and retrieval system, without the written consent of the authors.

This novella is a work of fiction. Names and characters are the product of the author's imagination. Any resemblance to actual living people, living or dead, is entirely coincidental.

V 1.2

Written by Sophie Brousseau & Chris Brousseau
Edited by: Sophie Brousseau
Cover image created by Benjamin Dawe
Super special thanks to Andrew Symons for his invaluable feedback and expert proofreading skills

Pirates of Nassau

About the Book

Pirates of Nassau is a five-part novella serial, set in the city of Nassau during the early 1700s. The story follows six main characters and their lives, during a time when pirates greatly outnumbered the local residents on this once tranquil isle.

Each novella forms an episode around seventy pages in length and when combined, they form a single novel.

Out now
Episode One: Turmoil
Episode Two: Betrayal
Episode Three: Greed
Episode Four: Deception
Episode Five: Reckoning

If you would like to stay up to date with our progress and release dates, sign up to our **email list**

Alternatively, you can find us all over social media
@maplelionfiction

*****

Warning! This book is intended for mature audiences. It has some violent scenes and mature language.
*****

About the Authors

Chris Brousseau hails from Timmins in Northern Canada. Having grown up in freezing temperatures he vowed to one day live in a hot sunny place and made the move to Melbourne, Australia in his mid-twenties, trading in man-eating bears and raccoons for venomous snakes and spiders. Chris has spent over a decade making video games, working on franchises such as The Sims and Need for Speed. He has transferred a lot of what he has learned along the way into his writing. From the process of managing creative endeavors through to character development and motivations. When he is not making or playing games, he spends his downtime writing fun fiction books with his wife Sophie.

At the age of nineteen, Sophie Brousseau set out on an international adventure. She traveled far from her home and birthplace of East Yorkshire, UK and wound up in Melbourne, Australia, where she still resides to this day, nearly two decades on. She recently returned to study, completing a degree in Psychological Sciences. It was here she honed her writing skills and whilst she found the subject matter fascinating, scientific writing wasn't her jam. Upon meeting her now husband Chris, they found they had a shared love of storytelling and decided to venture into the world of fiction writing together.

When they set out to write they found each naturally gravitated towards a different role. Chris is the creative mind who comes up with the initial story and characters for each book. Sophie then springs into action and further develops the world, injecting life into the characters using fancy words.

Pirates of Nassau

The Brousseau's love hearing from readers and can be contacted through email: maplelionfiction@gmail.com or follow along on Instagram @maplelionfiction, Twitter @maplelionwrites and Facebook @maplelionfiction where they share not only their finished product but the process it takes to make it. All of their books are published under Maple Lion Fiction. To find out more visit: maplelionfiction.com

Pirates of Nassau

A Pirate Novella Serial

By Sophie & Chris Brousseau

Previously in Pirates of Nassau

Captain Crow
After losing his quartermaster a devastated Crow seeks revenge. Not only does he slay the captain of the guard but he finally hunts down Johnny Ives; the man who stole his captaincy from him and tried to have him killed. Crow rescues a beaten down Isaac from Johnny's clutches and then takes matters into his own hands.

Molly Weaver
Molly's world is shattered when she discovers Jane Hatch's second in command, Thunder is in fact her long lost son, Daniel Weaver. Molly has already set the wheels in motion for Vella to attack Jane and her people, but rushes to stop this happening only to be attacked and captured by Jacky Boy, a vengeful brothel punter.

Jane Hatch
Having lost her one true friend, Jane hunts for answers only to find there is a traitor amongst her ranks and it's someone close to her too. As she makes preparations for the pressing war with Vella, Joy returns from her latest job and arouses Jane's suspicions. Jane accuses Joy of lying and is met with a paralyzing blade to the neck.

Joy Lafitte
After being ordered to kill Popino on behalf of Jane Hatch, Joy pays him a visit only to find a distraught Popino in a lot of trouble. His

Pirates of Nassau

daughter is missing and Joy vows to help get her back if he agrees to go into hiding until things with Jane are taken care of. Joy sends Popino off to Roy's place and returns to the merc mansion to take care of business. Once alone with Jane, Joy seizes the opportunity to strike and throws a paralyzing blade to the neck but her getaway is interrupted by Leon, who vows to help her but instead knocks her unconscious.

Isaac Carver

An imprisoned Isaac is rescued from a date with the gallows once again but this time at the hands of Johnny Ives and his motley crew. His rescue is bittersweet as he watches his new found friend Nelson die at the hands of Ives. Isaac is held at Vella's place, plied with rum and forced to help formulate an attack on Jane Hatch. It's here his old friend Popino hunts him down but when Johnny and Vella catch them together, they decide Isaac has had his use. All hope is lost until Crow comes to the rescue and Isaac is saved once again.

Popino Beltrame

A distraught Popino finds his young daughter, Rose, gone and their housekeeper dead. A note left behind suggests that Vella is to blame but after a visit from Joy, Popino is forced into hiding. When Joy fails to return, Popino takes matters into his own hands and searches Vella's property for Rose only to be chased off the property by Vella herself. He joins a civilian crew working for Jane Hatch with the plan to search Jane's place for Rose but Vella finally catches up with him and enacts her revenge, shooting Popino before her own life is ended.

Episode Five

Reckoning

Jane Hatch

Jane's eyeballs throbbed as her lids fluttered open. Not again. She closed her eyes and took a deep breath. Another fucking cell. She thought someone would have come to rescue her by now, but then, again given the amount of times they had moved her, nobody probably knew where to look. She pushed herself up to sitting, her hand slipped a little on the wet sludge covered floor.

Jane had been alone up until this point but now in the far corner lay Joy, curled up, out cold. In the neighboring cell lay a huge beast of an individual. They faced the wall and looked to be asleep. Jane couldn't see much other than some blood splatter throughout their mop of curly gray hair. She put her head in her hands. Her insides longed for a drink, just something to take the edge off. Even if Margaret were here, she'd understand she told herself. This was extreme circumstances. A familiar voice interrupted her thoughts.

"Shut the fuck up!" Jane recognized Leon's voice screaming in the hallway.

"Shut up Jack, you bastard!" Leon yelled.

"Prick," she muttered. She pushed herself to standing and pressed her head to the cell bars but couldn't make out much. She turned and looked to the small window at the top of the grimy wall. Maybe if she stuck her hand out someone might help. Maybe they'd then see who she was? She had no idea where she even was but it was worth a try.

She looked at Joy who lay disheveled and bruised, breathing softly. Jane tried to work out what she should do with her. If it wasn't for her, she wouldn't be in this mess in the first place, she thought.

"Wake up!" She gave Joy a shove with her boot.

Joy stirred. "Where am I?" She shielded her face with her arms. "Oh fuck." Joy scrambled to stand.

"Oh fuck indeed," Jane said. She wanted to be angrier than she was with Joy. "So, I finally get to speak to you."

Joy slid down the wall and crouched. Whatever they had given them had clearly knocked her around. "I nee... ded the coin okay." She slurred a little as she spoke.

"So I assumed. The bounty, you took it?" Jane said.

Joy nodded in reply.

"I ought to tear you limb from limb but, quite frankly, I don't have the energy; I'm going to save it to get out of this hellhole," Jane said and put her hands on her hips.

"And what makes you think I won't try anything?" Joy smirked.

Jane stormed over and grabbed Joy by the throat. "Because I could fucking strangle you to death right now, but I'm choosing not to." Jane dropped her grip. "You had your chance. You blew it."

Joy patted her pockets, her eyes still half shut.

"They've taken all our weapons so don't waste your time." Jane folded her arms and stared at her.

Joy opened her eyes fully and stared back at Jane. "My sister. I was doing it for my sister. Someone took her. Made her a slave." Joy let out a big breath. "There's a guy that knows who did it, and he'll tell me for fifteen doubloons. There was seven alone for bringing you in alive." Joy shook her head.

Jane remained silent. She couldn't deny she wouldn't have done the same, after all her entire business revolved around killing people for money. Her hands were hardly clean. "Well, you were brave to even try. I didn't think anyone would dare take that bounty on me." Jane tapped her hand on her folded arm. "You're a bit too impulsive though." She brushed at the wound on her neck. "Had to learn that lesson myself." Jane faced Joy. "Tell me, did you even kill Popino?"

"No." Joy put her head down. "His daughter's gone, y'know?"

Pirates of Nassau

"It doesn't surprise me. That slimy bastard owes coin all over the place."

"He's a charmer that one," Joy said.

"Don't fall for it." Jane pressed her lips together. "Look... I think we're stronger if we're together." She extended her hand to Joy. "Agreed?"

Joy's mouth fell open as she returned the handshake.

"What?" Jane asked.

"I'm just shocked that you would forgive me so easily," Joy said.

"Who said anything about forgiveness. But I'll certainly forget... for now." Jane couldn't help but smile at Joy. She reminded her so much of her younger self. "This business isn't for everyone. You can hold a grudge but not to your own detriment."

Joy stared at Jane. "I can't believe how composed you are. How do you do it? How do you keep it together?"

Jane shrugged. "Who says I am." She gave a wry smile. "Anyway." She clasped her hands together as if hoping to find strength. "I think I know the man you speak of. Not the one who kidnapped your sister but the one who knows his identity."

"What? How?" Joy cocked her head to the side.

"He works for me. Name's Grimm right?" Jane said.

Joy nodded.

"He told me about people coming to Nassau and stealing children. I wasn't sure whether to believe him. He's a bit of a... trickster. Talks a lot. It's hard to be sure what to believe with him, but he does know a lot of people so it's possible he has your information." Jane reached into her inside pocket and handed Joy a small button-sized coin with a fox head and three notches scratched into it. "Show this to anyone who works for me, and they'll do whatever you ask. They have to. Save you having to kill me to get your answers." Jane raised her eyebrows.

"I don't know what to say," Joy said and steadied herself on her feet.

"Just take it and help me get the hell out of here. I detest these places."

"I've never been in one," Joy said.

Pirates of Nassau

"Trust me, it's not somewhere you want to see again." Jane rubbed at her face with her palms. "Right, we've got to get out of here fast. I heard Leon screaming at someone before so he's still close by." Jane marched over to the window.

"I can't believe I ever trusted that fucker," Joy said.

"He had us both fooled." Jane shook her head and chewed at her lip.

"Give me a foot up, I'll try to stick my hand out. Grab someone's leg or something. Maybe we can bribe them?"

"Sure." Joy rushed over and knelt down to give Jane a boost.

They both froze at the sound of voices. "Put the girl in the cage. We'll sell her in Devils Cay later," the voice said.

Jane and Joy looked at one another, their eyes wide in horror.

"Now, now ladies. Don't be trying nothing here," Leon said as he walked into the room, a piece of steaming hot bread sitting on his hook and a glass in his good hand. He took a bite. "I'm glad you're finally awake. I'd missed you."

"Fuck you!" Jane curled her fists into balls.

Leon smiled then took a bite of the bread. "You know, I still can't believe I managed to fool you for so long." Leon took a seat. "I mean, you really trusted me. And you're normally so good at reading people. You pride yourself on your judgment. Jane Hatch, the famous mind reader."

Jane's face grew hot. She wanted to scream. She wanted to smash his head into that table. Tear that hook clean off.

"How many years have we been together?" Leon smirked.

"Fuck. You." Jane turned her back on him. She needed to think. To block out his drivel.

"And my beautiful Joy. Thank you for setting up this opportunity for me. I've been waiting years, but there was never a right time. Too risky. But then you came along and just did half the work for me." He took another bite of the bread. "Never thought you'd be charmed by an old hook hand but you don't seem to be too picky." He shot Joy a wink.

Joy dusted herself off and stood at the bars. "You're very good, Leon. Had me going."

Pirates of Nassau

Jane watched as Joy pulled down her top a little and bent over. "Maybe we could be a team?" Joy shot him a wink back.

Leon stared as if mesmerized. "Nup, nah. Not falling for it!" Leon said.

"Don't waste your time on that no cocked waste of air, Joy," Jane said.

"Worth a try." Joy shrugged.

Jane paced the cell. "What is it you want?"

"Me?" Leon placed his hand on his chest. "I don't want for much, but the boss on the other hand..."

Jane put her face as close to the bars as possible and eyed Leon's reactions. "And who's that? Who's your boss? Vella?"

"Pf, please. She's half cracked! I think she's slaying your people as we speak though, so not all bad."

"Is it Thad then?" Jane narrowed her gaze and honed in on Leon's face. "It's Thad isn't it?"

"Wrong again! You're really not good at this. Thad's right there." Leon pointed to the neighboring cell.

Jane stared at the huge lifeless body. "No!" Jane covered her mouth. "I can't believe after all these years I'm finally looking at him."

"That's Thad?" Joy walked over to the other side of the cell and peered through the bars. "He's huge!"

"She," Leon corrected. "Thad's a woman. Goes by the name of Molly. Not quite so intimidating, is it?" Leon laughed.

Jane glared in Leon's direction. "Makes sense. Of course Nassau is run by women. So the question is, who do you work for then?" Jane poked her tongue in her cheek. She hated not knowing.

"The Boss."

"Their name is, 'Boss'?" Jane asked.

"Yup." Leon took a sip of his drink. "Boss wants you all out of the picture. You, Vella, Thad." Leon rolled his eyes at the mention of the last name. "Can't believe we've pulled it off!"

"I wouldn't be so quick to celebrate," Jane said.

"Still feisty, even when you're locked up with no way out. Still got that spark, I always did admire that in you." Leon looked into his cup. "And you thought I was just a sad cripple."

"I wouldn't have hired you if I thought that, Leon," Jane said. She tried her best to stay calm as her eyes searched for a way out. Something. Anything. She looked back at Leon. Every sip he took infuriated her. Her temper flared.

"Did you kill Margaret?" She knew the answer, but she needed to hear the words from him.

Leon gave a telling smile.

"How fucking could you!" Jane screamed. "You piece of fucking shit. She trusted you. She was nothing but kind. You should have kept her out of it." Jane grabbed at the cell bars and started to shake them. "Let me fucking out of here you, you..." Jane felt a hand on her shoulder.

"Save it." Joy caught her eye.

Leon stood up and tapped his cup against the bars. "Looks like I need a top up!"

Jane stuck her arms through and reached out to grab him. Leon dodged her grasp.

"I've been working for the Boss for years. Slowly sabotaging you." Leon reached into his baggy tan waistcoat and pulled out a flask. "Remember during the raid on Nassau?" He took a sip and tried to speak but choked a little. "Few of your best went missing there." Leon gave a nod.

Jane pulled at the bars, as if trying to pry them apart. He'd been under her nose all this time. She could have stopped him. She could have saved Margaret.

Leon took another sip from the flask and started to cough. "Phew, that... tastes awful." Leon winced.

"You're more fucked up than I ever imagined," Joy said and stood by Jane's side.

"I'll take that as a compliment. I mean you both kill people for a living too." Leon returned to his chair. "Business is business. The Boss wanted me to cause trouble for you, so I did. He paid me. You also paid me. It's nothing personal."

"It is fucking personal when you lie to me and kill my people!" Jane screamed. She dropped to the ground and unlaced her weighty black boot then hurled it through the bars. The boot hit Leon square in the face. He sat stunned.

Joy let out a laugh. "Ha! Good one."

"Well, well, well, quite the mouth on you. I didn't expect that." A tall man strode into the room. He wore a beautiful black captain's jacket and a striking red and black tricorn hat. In his hand he held an embossed black wood flintlock.

"And who the fuck are you?" Jane said.

"So feisty." He smiled revealing a missing front tooth.

She eyed him as he paraded in front of her cell with a swagger in his stride. He sported the confidence of a far better looking man and Jane got the impression he thought himself charming, but in truth he came off as nothing but creepy and smug.

"I'm the one you've been hearing about. The Boss." He turned to face her.

"The Boss of what? Bunch of bitches?" Jane waved her finger in the direction of Leon.

"That's funny." He laughed and it quickly turned into a sneer as he leered through the cell bars. "You're both very easy on the eye aren't you."

"She's not with me. Leave her out of this," Jane said and pointed in Joy's direction.

"I've been trying to get you for years you know," the Boss said.

Jane wracked her brains. Did she know this man from somewhere? There didn't look to be anything familiar about him. She noticed a gold snake pinned to his jacket lapel. What family did it belong to? Someone in Nassau? She pondered as he peered in at her.

"And how lucky of us to have captured the infamous Thad too." The Boss walked over to Molly's cell. "What a giant of a human. Surprised she's still sleeping though."

"Yeah, I'm not." Jacky Boy limped into the room and waggled a small brown bottle. "We gave her a triple dose. She's as strong as ten men. Old bitch." He gave a slow nod and fixed his gaze on Jane. "I see our entertainment's awake."

Jane recoiled at his words. He was a grimy man with a peg leg and oozed sleaze.

Pirates of Nassau

"Keep a lid on it, Jacky Boy. These two will have your dick off!" The Boss smirked and stroked at his chin. "What shall we do with them boys?"

The three men grinned and leered at Jane and Joy. Jane had been in a lot of bad situations with a lot of bad people but something told her she wasn't getting out of this one unharmed.

"Who even are you?" Jane stared at the men. "Why hide behind a name?"

"I don't. Just a nickname," the Boss said.

Jane thought about what she could do to get herself out of this situation. She heard Joy shuffling about behind her and hoped she had figured something out. She'd keep them talking. Keep them distracted.

"What's with the snake?" Jane asked.

The Boss walked over and pushed his face against hers through the bars. "So many questions."

His eyes blazed with a venomous hate. He seemed aggravated and clearly didn't like questions. She'd bargain with him instead, though it was hard to tell what a man like this wanted other than power and right now he had a lot of that.

He raised his flintlock and pushed it through the bar and into her chest. Typical man relying on weapons to solve problems she thought. She'd use her brain to get out of this just like she always did. He pressed the barrel into her harder and glared. She needed to bargain and fast. "I have a lot of resources at my disposal you know. Coin too. What's say we strike a deal? Team up even? Wouldn't you like an army of mercenaries at your command?"

His glare didn't falter.

"What is it you want? Land? How about the mansion?"

"Too many questions." He pulled the trigger and the deafening snap bounced off the walls as blood splatter erupted and Jane's body slumped to the ground.

Molly Weaver

The snap of gunfire awoke Molly from her heavy slumber. She peeled her face away from the grimy floor which smelt worse than the dock. "What's going on?" she mumbled and cleared her throat. Her wounded leg throbbed and her entire body ached. She pushed herself up to sitting and fought off a wave of nausea. Her eyes fixed on a man dusting off a black wood pistol. A woman's body lay on the ground in the next cell surrounded by a puddle of blood and a brown-haired woman stood pressed into the corner, staring at the lifeless body.

"You! You bastard!" the brown-haired woman yelled.

"Boss! Look who's awake."

Molly rolled her eyes. "Jacky Boy." She sighed. "Seems I'll be forever haunted by you and that peg leg. Pff." Molly smirked. "What a joke."

The pistol-toting man strode over to Molly's cell. He wore a black and red captain's jacket with a matching three-cornered hat. "How the mighty Thad has fallen," he said. His gruff voice was surprisingly eloquent.

"I'd let me out of here quick smart if I were you," Molly said.

"Why would we do that? You don't scare us!" Jacky Boy peered through the grubby bars.

Molly stomped over and made a grab for him. He wobbled backwards.

Pirates of Nassau

"Ha! Missed!" Jacky Boy taunted.

His spiteful whiny voice wound Molly up. She gripped the cell bars tight. "Let me out of here or you'll be sorry!" She tried with all her might to pry the bars apart, to move or twist them just an inch, but nothing. She released her grip and counted in her head. Don't let them see they've got to you, she told herself. "You'll pay," she said under her breath as she turned away. The exertion made her leg throb harder. She looked down at the wound which they had cleaned up for her. Though she wasn't sure why they'd bother.

"Now, now Thad, or is it Molly? It's very confusing. What shall we call you?" The black and red-hatted man asked as he holstered his pistol.

"Whatever," Molly said and walked to the back of the cell. She needed a way out. If she played nice for now, maybe they would let their guard down. Maybe that brown haired girl would help her. "Molly, call me Molly." She strained to sound remotely pleasant. She peered into the other cell. "Was that Jane Hatch?"

"Certainly was. I've been waiting years to get my hands on you lot," the man said. He interlaced his fingers and cracked them. "You made my job difficult, I'll give you that much. You're sneaky." He nodded as if impressed and flashed Molly a devious smile which revealed a missing front tooth.

She stared at his crinkled face. There was a familiarity about it that she couldn't shake. Her eyes jumped to his jacket and stopped at the lapel which had a small golden object pinned to it.

"What's on your jacket?" Molly asked.

"Ha, never you mind." He brushed his hand against the pin.

"Do you have a name?" Molly pushed. She needed information. Something to help piece this puzzle together.

"I'm, the Boss." He put his hand to his chest and gave a little bow. His tanned skin crinkled as he spoke.

"Right. Well, that's as clear as mud. Care to elaborate?" Molly said.

"Ha! Haven't heard that one before. I'm surprised you don't know me."

"That makes two of us," Molly muttered to herself.

Pirates of Nassau

"Do you like your new lodgings? Rather nice isn't it," he said and flung his arms in the air.

"It's disgusting, as it's no doubt intended to be," Molly replied. She looked over at Jane. "Whoever killed her should go see Roy. There'll be some doubloons waiting from me."

"Roy?" The brown-haired woman in the corner shot Molly a glare. "How do you know Roy?"

"Who are you?" Molly nodded and turned away from the Boss and his men.

"Joy. Lafitte."

"Ah yes, Roy told me about you." She nodded. "Shame you've ended up here, but take the credit for this one when you get out." Molly pointed towards Jane.

"Ha! You're not going anywhere! Neither of you!" Jacky Boy stood at Joy's cell door and licked his lips.

"We'll see," Joy said.

"Aw don't you want to stay with us, Joy? I thought you liked me," a man with a hook hand sauntered through the door and shot Joy a wink.

"Who'd like you?" Molly said and took a seat on the sludge covered floor. Her leg blazed with pain.

"Now, now, Molly, Leon has many redeeming qualities!" the Boss said.

Jacky Boy hobbled over to Molly's cell door. He gripped the bars and stared in. "Did you get my messages?"

"Maybe?" Molly said and shrugged.

"Those severed tongues in boxes, that was me," Jacky Boy said.

"Bravo," Molly said and looked over to Joy. She rolled her eyes. "Truly terrifying... clearly."

"Why can't we just kill her! You miserable old cow. I should have shot you myself, finished the job off!" Jacky Boy yelled.

"Enough!" The Boss raised a hand. "Make yourself comfortable Molly. You're going to be here for a while. Can't kill you just yet." He flashed a wicked grin in her direction and made for the door.

Molly ignored his attempt to scare her and instead cast her mind back to where she might know him from. That smile of his was all too familiar.

"We'll leave you with Jacky Boy, he'll take good care of you until I return. I've got some... questions I need answered." He cracked his knuckles. "Don't let her out of your sight. And figure a way to clean up that mess." The Boss waved his finger in Jane's direction. Leon followed him out and closed the clunky, thick door behind them.

"Yes, sir," Jacky Boy said and slapped his thigh with glee. "Look who's in charge now! Me!"

Molly shook her head and peaked through the bars at Joy. She looked shaken. "You okay?" she asked.

Joy walked over and pressed her head into the bars which separated the two cells. "I can't believe he killed her. It was so quick."

"I thought you wanted her dead? I know I did." Molly shrugged. "When you kill people for a living, you can't expect that others won't do the same."

Joy puffed out her cheeks and let out a loud gasp of air.

"You liked her, didn't you?" Molly said.

Joy cleared her throat and avoided Molly's gaze. "I think they've got children here. In cages."

"Shut it!" Jacky Boy yelled.

His voice infuriated Molly. She eyed her surroundings. The small window in the corner of Joy's cell suggested they were at least close to the outside world. She paused and listened. The hum of bugs which surfaced at night had started up. Molly's eyes shot to her satchel, dumped in the corner of the room.

"Found anything good in my bag, Jacky Boy?" She wasn't going to waste her energy giving him the reaction he expected.

"What bag?"

"That brown leather one in the corner." Molly nodded her head. She wondered if he was really so stupid that he hadn't even checked the contents.

He looked at the bag but didn't move.

"Ha! Are you scared of touching it, floppy boy?" Molly said.

Pirates of Nassau

"I'm not scared of nothing." He snatched up the bag and tipped the contents on the ground.

"Think your boss might be interested in that bit of paper." Molly raised her brows.

He grabbed the worn piece of parchment and fumbled to unfold the tattered edges.

"Careful now, it's very old," Molly said.

"Half a map!" he rushed to the door and wobbled away down the corridor.

"Hey! Boss!" he yelled.

Molly's ears pricked up at the sound of faint cries. They sounded like those of a child.

"Hear that?" Joy ran to the cell door. "I can't stand it," she said and covered her mouth.

"Shh!" Molly put her hand to her lips and pushed herself to standing. "Listen." Molly pointed toward the corridor.

"Boss, come here!" Jacky Boy yelled.

Molly bent down on one knee. Hot pain seared through her injured leg. She braced as she stuck her hand through the grubby bars and tried to grab her bag. The strap lay inches away from her grasp. She prized her arm through. Further and further but to no avail.

"Oi!" Jacky Boy yelled. He wobbled back in the room and lunged at Molly's arm.

She pulled it back fast. The snug fit of the bars tore at her skin. "Fuck!" Molly said through gritted teeth.

The Boss strode into the room. "What is it?"

"A map." Jacky Boy thrust the paper into the Bosses hand.

The Boss lifted the tattered map close to the candle light. "C. Kidd. Treasure not found." His eyes lit up. "Oh, this is good." He scoured the parchment. "But where's the rest of it? There's only half here!" The Boss scowled at Molly.

"That's all I've got for now but I have it on good authority that the other half is complete and I just so happen to know where to find it. That's Captain Kidd's treasure you know?"

"Is that right?" The Boss grinned.

"If you let me out of here, I can take you to it?" Molly said in her nicest voice.

Leon came through the door. "What is it?"

"Half a map, apparently Thad knows where the other half is too!" Jacky Boy said.

"Oh sure. And what, we just need to let her out and she can show us where it is. Pff. I don't think so!" Leon said.

"You hook-handed little fuck!" Molly said under her breath.

"Don't be so hasty Leon. I think we might be talking about Captain Kidd's thirty thousand doubloons." The Boss tapped his tanned leathery finger on his chin. "I'll think about it. But for now make the preparations for Devils Cay, we need to set sail soon."

"Tide's about to turn you know," Leon said.

"Then quickly, load the children on and make sure you get that pretty young thing. She'll fetch a lot. He'll be pleased." The Boss smirked.

"The Beltrame kid?" Leon asked.

"Beltrame?" Joy grabbed the bars. "Do they all go to Devil's Cay? Is that where you take them? Is that where you took Raven, you sick pieces of shit!" She shook the bars and screamed. "Let me out, you fucks!"

"Shut her up, Jacky Boy! She's annoying me," The Boss said.

"Can't I start torturing this one first?" Jacky Boy looked to Molly, his eyes filled with a lust for vengeance.

"Soon enough. Needs to weaken a little first and I'm sure a few more days without food will help with that," The Boss said and walked out with Leon who slammed the door behind them.

Jacky Boy turned to Molly and gave a chuckle. "Who'd of thought I'd be the one in charge of you. Should have let me have my fun that day shouldn't you."

"What say we strike a deal?" Molly said and clenched her jaw. She loathed being nice to this prick. "Just you and me this time."

Joy shot Molly a look of confusion.

"How about I give you another bit of treasure and in exchange, you give me some food?" Molly tried to make her voice sound somewhat pleasant though it pained her.

Pirates of Nassau

"Not gonna give me my leg back is it, cow!"

Molly tried to hide her smirk. "Just grab yourself that clam shell."

Jacky Boy gave the shell a poke with his boot. "What is it?"

"I use them to smuggle jewelry. Inside is a very expensive ring that would fetch a pretty price." Molly pointed and nodded in encouragement.

"You want to give me this ring in exchange for a bit of food? Don't make sense."

"Well, I don't have a choice do I! I'm hungry!" Molly yelled. She stood up and pulled out her handkerchief.

"You gonna cry?" Jacky Boy laughed.

"Just stomp on the fucking clam to open it. The ring's yours." Molly turned away and feigned a sigh filled with sorrow.

A stomp, a crack and a crunch followed.

Boom.

The room erupted in smoke. Molly pressed the handkerchief over her face and burrowed her head into the wall.

Coughs came from Joy's cell.

Molly waited a moment then tucked her handkerchief away, squeezed her eyes tight shut and fumbled for the bars. Her hands landed on the rough iron. She patted them down hoping for a gap, but they were all still in place. She pulled one, then another. They were at least looser than before. She made her way down the row, shaking each in turn until her hand stopped on one that moved a lot. She gave the bar a yank and it came clean out. She sniffed the air. The smoke seemed to have dissipated. She peaked through one eye. Jacky Boy lay at her feet. Bloodied and at the least unconscious. Dead she hoped. She looked to Joy who was following her lead and shaking at the bars but with no luck. She reached into Jacky Boy's pockets and found a set of keys then tossed them into Joy's cell. "I've done my part."

Joy grabbed the keys. "Fuck! Fine."

Molly grabbed her satchel and scrambled for the unlocked door. Ahead lay a dimly lit corridor with a ceiling so low she could touch the roof with her hand. She limped down it, gritting her teeth to bare the pain of her wounded leg. Her body tensed. Not only with the pain but the suffocating small space. As she crept down the corridor her ears pricked up. She could hear those muffled cries again. Those of a child. It sickened her. The people she dealt with had chosen this life. They wanted the riches, they wanted the power but these children didn't ask to be dragged into this mess. They were innocent. She'd been innocent. Her mind cast back to sobbing on the street, being kicked, beaten and starved like an unwanted dog. She'd never fought back. She didn't have the strength, but now it was a different story.

She listened intently and located the cries. She hobbled over and pressed her ear to the door. The muffled sobs were on the other side. A surge of adrenaline rushed through her. She smashed her weight into the door and burst into the room.

"What in the...?" Two guards stared at her in shock. They sat atop a six-foot-long cage. The room was filled with them, all stacked upon one another. Inside, children cowered, a couple in each.

"You bastards!" Molly grabbed them both by the neck and smashed their heads together, knocking them out.

She closed the door behind her and held her breath as footsteps rushed by. They rushed past in the direction of the cells. She didn't have much time. She put her finger to her lips and motioned for the children to be quiet. Their frightened eyes made her heart heavy. "It's okay," she whispered. "We'll all get out of here."

She searched the guards' pockets for the keys. "Yes!" Her hand struck a heap on a rope. She frantically unlocked the cages. "Be quiet, follow me and stay close."

They reached out for her hands and clung to any body part they could. "Okay, you can't all grab onto me. Hold each other's hands down the corridor then we run," she whispered and listened at the door. Clangs of swords and screams followed but they at least seemed distant. She peeled open the door and poked her head out. They all looked to be busy with Joy. In the other direction the corridor stretched far but no one was in sight. She opened the door and waved the children through. "Follow me." She led the way and broke into a hobbled run. The children stayed close behind. They reached a large room filled with tables on which abandoned plates of food and jugs of drink sat. To the right-hand side there was a large door which Molly assumed led to the outside world. A small boy with a dirty tear-stained face tugged at her sleeve. He couldn't have been more than six or seven years old.

"I came through here." He pointed to the door.

"Does it go outside?" Molly asked.

He nodded in response.

"Excellent." Molly put her arms out and herded the children together. "Now I'm going to open that door and if the men are on the other side I want you to run as far as you can from here and don't look back." Molly nodded. Their eyes were filled with terror. "I'll take care of anyone who gets in our way, okay?"

They nodded and gripped any part of her they could.

"You need to let go of me, be brave, one last time," Molly said and crept forward.

She reached the heavy door and heaved it open, ready to face an army of men. Nothing. She ushered the children outside. In the far distance she made out what she assumed to be the city of Nassau. She'd never ventured this far. There was no reason to, there was nothing here. Or at least so she thought.

Molly signaled with her hand for the children to follow her. They ran toward a dark leaf filled-field and hid amongst the foliage. Through the otherwise still night she could hear a ship being loaded. They hadn't been missed yet. She turned to the children. The fear in their eyes had receded slightly. "Now, we've a long walk ahead of us, but we're free!" Molly said. It would be a slow half day walk back to town through the rough fields of palms, but she was free. They were free.

Captain Crow

Crow stood in the grassy valley and cast his eyes over the carnage. Lifeless bodies littered the ground around him. Johnny's included. The sky rumbled and the breeze picked up. His eyes moved upwards to the pockets of smoke which now swirled in with the clouds creating a thick heavy sky.

"What's happening beyond the mound, boy?" he asked Isaac whose back was to him with his head focused down. "What you looking at?"

"Nothing." Isaac turned to face him and tucked something away in his pocket. "Jane Hatch's people are at war with Vella."

"Then let's go help her." Crow turned to his men and nodded. "Boy?"

Isaac scrunched up his face. "Vella? Why?" he asked. "I say we finally go find that treasure!" Isaac rubbed his hands together. "You with me fellas?" He patted down a couple of the bodies at his feet. "Besides, I'm not sure she'll want my help."

A few of the men's eyes lit up at the mention of treasure.

"We owe her!" Crow was so used to including Nelson in everything he said.

"Well, I owe her. Nelson and I struck a deal," Crow raised his voice.

"I see. Guess me being kidnapped and held by her doesn't matter." Isaac's hand landed on a flask. "Finally!" He tipped the contents into his mouth.

Pirates of Nassau

Crow stormed over and stuck his face inches away from Isaac's. "We made a deal okay and I don't go back on my word."

Isaac rolled his eyes. "What's to stop her killing me down there?" he said and tossed the empty flask.

"Me!" Crow's gaze didn't falter. He made sure his eyes burned into Isaac's.

"Okay." Isaac sighed. "Guess you did just save me from that prick."

"Exactly." Crow turned to face his men who had drawn their weapons, ready to charge.

"Men! Stay clear of any women with dreadlocked hair or V's stamped on their jackets. They're Vella's girls. Take out anyone else. Then we'll get V onside and get that treasure." He raised a blade and pistol above his head. "You with me?"

"Yes, Captain!" the men cheered.

They ran up the grassy mound and stood on top. Below, swarms of people were hacking and slashing at anything in sight.

"We run down on my command." Crow scanned the grounds of the infamous merc mansion, his eyes searched for Vella. He saw the bizarre wooden structure she'd been building for so long but never used. It was empty. The smoke-filled air made it difficult to make out anyone clearly. A flurry of cannonballs shot through the air and erupted. Bodies tumbled and smashed down into the mud.

"Are we sure we want to go down there?" Isaac said.

"We're no cowards!" Crow said. "Right, men?"

"Yes, Captain," the men agreed.

Crow raised his pistol in the air. "Go!" Crow yelled and charged down the hill. The men hurtled down with him, Isaac included.

It hadn't looked far but it seemed to take forever to reach the bottom, and when they finally did, the fire stopped. Bodies lay bleeding out in the muddy earth. "We're too late." Crow panicked, his eyes searched for Vella. Not again, he thought to himself. I'm always too late. Thoughts of Nelson pricked at his mind.

"Over there!" Isaac said and pointed, interrupting Crow's thoughts.

A huge man stood over Vella with a spear raised above her. Next to him stood a smaller man. "No!" Crow yelled and ran toward them as fast as his legs would carry him. He needed to be closer to have a clear shot.

"Pino!" Isaac yelled and sprinted towards the men. "It's Popino!"

Crow couldn't get there fast enough. He watched as Vella raised her arm and shot. The smaller man flew backward with the impact.

"No!" Isaac screamed.

"You bitch!" The huge man slammed his spear down into Vella.

Crow stopped dead and shot. The huge man dropped to his knees. The snap of gun fire carried through the air. Isaac sprinted past and dragged the body of the smaller man away. Crow ran over to the huge man who rolled on the ground in pain. He looked at Vella. Her thick hair was matted with clumps of dirt and blood. The handle of the huge spear which had ended it all stuck out from her chest. A few paces away Isaac cradled the smaller man's head in his arms and rocked. A hand reached out for Crow's ankle. "I don't think so." Crow kicked the huge man's meaty hand away. "I should keep you alive, make you suffer!"

"What shall we do with him, Captain?" Several of Crow's men caught up and stood by his side. Others had run off and were checking bodies for weapons and loot.

"Think we can get any coin for him? Is there even anyone left to bribe?" Crow said.

The men shrugged.

Crow lifted a flintlock pistol to end him. He aimed and cocked the gun.

"Oi! Old man! Leave him the fuck alone!" A man wearing a black bandana sprinted toward him, closely followed by a thin-faced weathered woman with a limp. She clutched a blade in one hand and used the other to help push her leg forward.

"Move any closer and I shoot," Crow said. He caught sight of Vella's butchered body. "On second thoughts." Crow pulled the trigger. The huge man stopped moving.

"Thunder!" The man with the black bandana yelled and ran at Crow. He flew into him with full force and knocked him to the ground. He raised his fist to pummel Crow but several pairs of hands dragged him off.

Pirates of Nassau

Crow scrambled to his feet. His men had the black bandana wearing man in a headlock. Three others had managed to tackle the weathered woman to the ground. "Take care of them. Both of them."

"No!" The bandana-wearing man cried out and tried to break free. He was met with a blade to the throat.

"I'll see you in hell!" The woman let out a cackle before one of Crow's men struck a blade through her back.

Crow reloaded his pistol and unloaded another shot into the huge man just to be sure. He walked over to Isaac. "Leave him boy," Crow said.

Isaac looked up. Tears pooled in his eyes. "This is my fault. I'm sorry Pino." He held his friend's head and didn't move.

Crow knelt down. He noticed a soft movement of the man's chest. "That wound, just the one in his side?" Crow asked. He checked Popino's body. He wasn't injured anywhere else.

"I don't know, maybe?" Isaac replied.

Crow put his hand to Popino's neck. "I can still feel movement. His blood's still going."

"What?" Isaac said.

"He's still alive! We need to block that gash though. Won't be for long otherwise. Give me your shirt."

Isaac ripped at his shirt. It was fairly tattered so the cloth tore easily. "This do?"

Crow took the tattered strips and bunched them up. He pushed them into the wound. "Men! We need to get this one out of here. Bring Vella too."

"But? She's gone." Isaac said.

"I know boy, but she deserves a proper burial. Let's take her home. Her girls will see we've helped and let us shelter there," Crow said and got to his feet. The men rallied around him and hoisted Popino up. His men. His tough old heart filled with pride. "You keep the pressure on that wound, boy. I'll lead the way."

Joy Lafitte

Joy's stomach rumbled and her feet throbbed. She still couldn't believe she'd made it out of that place alive. She wondered if Molly had too. No one had bothered to come after her which suggested they'd either got what they wanted and captured the mighty Thad or were too busy shipping off those poor children. Her stomach knotted at the thought. She still didn't know who in Devils Cay wanted them, but at least she now knew where to look.

As she trudged through yet another field, she was grateful for the tall palms which sheltered her from the sweltering heat. In the distance, heads of people working in the fields bobbed up and down. The center of Nassau wasn't far away now. Her body longed to head straight for home but the vengeance in her heart wouldn't let her rest.

She dug inside her pocket and her fingers brushed the small silver coin Jane had given her. She hoped what Jane had told her was true. Her hand struck what she had been looking for, a thick brass object which she had taken from Jane's jacket before making her escape. The coin-shaped piece caught the sun and the glint lit up the word, 'Hatch'. Joy assumed it to be a sort of family medallion and tucked it back away for safekeeping.

She reached the outskirts of town and made for the center square. First stop would be a visit to Grimm, and Joy knew exactly where to find him. Up ahead she noticed a crowd of people gathered. He would no doubt be in the middle. She pushed her way through and spied his typical set up: cards on the table and heavy-bosomed women with low cut tops to distract the men. The sight of his smug face enraged her. She barged her way to the front and slammed her hands down on the table. "I want a word with you!"

"My! My!" Grimm said taken aback not only by the interruption but probably by Joy's appearance too. She rarely looked so disheveled.

"Sod off! I was just about to win!" A small grimy man gave her a push.

"Now, now! There's plenty of winnings for everyone!" Grimm gave his best beaming showman's smile. "Joy, dear, if you wouldn't mind stepping aside. I'll give you my full attention in a moment." He shot her a wink and didn't move his gaze from hers until she gave a roll of her eyes.

She wanted to push his stupid table over, snap off one of the legs and hit him over the head. Why wouldn't he just give her the information? Why did he even need payment? Did he not care about those children? Joy stepped aside and tapped her foot. Either way he was gutless or greedy or both, and she hated that she needed something from him.

"Alright gentlemen, I've got seventeen, what do you want to do?" Grimm's smile widened as he tapped his long skinny finger on the table.

Joy kept her eyes fixed on him. He looked so smarmy and sly. He always did. His sharp thin black mustache joined up with an unusually well-groomed beard. He wore a near immaculate black waistcoat with a crisp white undershirt. Who could keep anything white that clean? Joy thought. She tried to work out if it was his face or his pristine clothing that annoyed her and decided it was both.

To the left of the table stood an oaf of a man with his arm draped around one of the hired busty women. The small grimy man who'd given Joy a push stood in the middle, rubbing his hands together. To Joy's surprise an impeccably dressed woman stood to the right. She wore a beautiful red, almost orange, long flowing dress trimmed with exquisite black lace. Surely she wouldn't be fooled by Grimm's antics, though to be fair, he did have a charm that people seemed to be lured in by. Joy never dabbled in cards but had observed many a game. Grimm always played twenty-one which seemed simple enough. Your cards just needed to total as near to twenty-one as possible without going over.

Joy counted. The small grimy man had nineteen but the confidence of someone with more.

"Good lady, what would you like to do?" Grimm smiled and leaned in towards the well-dressed woman.

"I'll hold off," the impeccably dressed woman said. Joy peaked over her shoulder. Her cards totaled twenty.

"Hit me." The big oaf tapped on his card. His hand added up to seventeen.

"Finally, some action." Grimm raised his eyebrows and hovered his hands over the card to build the anticipation. He flipped a new card over and pushed it toward the big oaf. "A ten, ooh, unlucky."

The oaf smacked his fist down on the table and scattered some reale in Grimm's direction. "I always lose with you!"

"Well, that's not true. Look at that beauty you're holding on to," Grimm said. "It's not all about the coin. Though, come back tomorrow and maybe you can have both." Grimm shot him a wink and turned to the remaining two players. "What would you like to do sir?"

The small grimy man looked overly confident. "I'll go another."

Grimm flipped a fresh card over. "Ooh an ace. You're at twenty."

"Very good for you," Grimm said and hovered his hand over the deck. He peaked down at his own cards which Joy added up to be seventeen. "Let's see, my turn." Grimm took his time taking out his card. Joy watched closely. The crowd leaned in with anticipation. "Twenty-one!" He smiled. "A four, what are the chances! Well, about two, point four percent actually but no one cares about that. Ha!"

"Aaaah, damn." The impeccably dressed woman tossed her money at Grimm and walked away.

"You!" The small grimy man shook his fist and stormed off.

Grimm scraped the coins across the table toward him. "Same time tomorrow good people." He scooped the coins into a pouch as the crowd dissipated then gathered the cards and slotted them away into a leather container.

Pirates of Nassau

"Finally!" Joy stepped toward him and stood with her hands on her hips.

"Joy, so nice to see you." Grimm looked her up and down. "Looking a bit worse for wear though, everything okay?" Grimm placed his items into a leather bag. He paused and waited for a response. "I assume you have the doubloons?" He folded his table down and snapped the latches shut.

"Better," Joy said.

Grimm's brow raised. "Really? Follow me then." He walked down a nearby alleyway and checked back over his shoulder every few steps. "This should be interesting," he said under his breath.

Joy followed him down the familiar path until they reached an unassuming doorway. Grimm unlocked the small wooden door and placed his items inside. He held the door open for Joy and bowed his head, "After you my dear."

"Thanks." Joy scanned the dark stone walls and stepped in. The cool inside temperature came as a welcome relief. She had been here only once before but recalled the place well. The room ahead was adorned with crimson drapes, plump comfortable seats and numerous candle-filled lanterns. A large woolen floor covering sat in the middle of the room with two long seats at either side. These were rare pieces of furniture for most people in Nassau. Joy's eyes stopped on a small figure perched on the long seat, eating. "Roy?" She couldn't believe her eyes. "Why are you here?" Joy turned quickly and checked over her shoulder.

"It's okay, Joy. Roy and I are old acquaintances," Grimm replied.

"You look exhausted, Joy," Roy said.

Joy's mouth fell open. She shook her head and hoped her eyes deceived her. She blinked a few times but nothing changed.

"Joy?" Roy said.

Joy walked toward Roy. "I think you failed to mention you knew one another." She balled her hands tight. She felt foolish to have ever trusted Roy. He was well aware of her situation and he had sat there and pretended to not even know Grimm's name.

"Well, you never asked," Roy said in between mouthfuls. Crumbs spilled down his front as he nibbled on what looked like some sort of biscuit.

Joy nodded. "I see."

"It's business, Joy. You know that," Roy said.

She took a seat opposite Roy. He looked away and shifted awkwardly.

Grimm clapped his hands together. "Well, now those awkward introductions are out the way let's get down to business." Grimm walked over to a cupboard and retrieved a tin and a bottle. He returned to where Joy and Roy were sitting and tipped some of the contents onto the table.

"More biscuits! Thank you, Grimm," Roy said and reached for another. "Try one Joy, they're delightful."

"I think you need a drink?" Grimm said.

Joy nodded. She couldn't find the words right now.

Grimm ripped the cork out from the bottle and poured her a glass. Her hand shook a little as she raised the receptacle to her mouth. She hadn't realized until now just how thirsty she was. Joy leaned forward, grabbed a biscuit and took a bite. She savored the unusual sweetness and washed it down with the sweet brown liquid. "I've got news for both of you."

"Exactly what I wanted to hear!" Roy smiled.

"Jane's dead," Joy said and displayed the Hatch brass coin in her hand.

"Well done! I knew you could do it," Roy said.

"Why didn't you tell me it was Thad who put out the hit on her?"

"Oh." Roy sat back and scratched the back of his head. "Joy... you know I do business with whoever gives me money."

"Yeah, but Thad? Well, Molly," Joy said.

"You found that out too? You have been busy," Roy replied.

Joy remained quiet and instead stared at Roy with fire in her eyes. He busied himself and fumbled with his satchel fastening. "It's just business Joy, please don't take offense." He retrieved five doubloons and extended his hand out to Joy with the coins. "Your pay, plus a little extra." His hand shook a little as he waited for Joy to take them.

"Thanks." She scooped them off his palm and didn't take her eyes off him.

"No, thank you." He smiled and brushed the crumbs from his front.

"So..." Roy tipped his head toward Grimm. "Ask! You have enough now."

"Oh." Grimm sat back. "You know about that, Roy?"

"I know a lot of things." Roy put his satchel strap over his head and hopped down off the seat.

"What happened to Popino, Roy?" Joy said.

"Oh yes, let's see. I sent him off to hide, and then he vanished," Roy replied and gave a shrug.

Joy wasn't sure what to make of that comment. She hoped Popino simply got tired of waiting and left of his own accord but Roy made it sound more sinister. Everything he said sounded sinister now.

"It was a pleasure doing business with you both but I must head off. Grimm, the package is on your bed." Roy made his way to the door, he paused for a moment and turned to Joy. "I heard that Isaac character you're friendly with is over at Vella's. The battle is done. Seems both Jane and Vella lost." Roy gave a chuckle. "Then again, Jane's entire place has been looted and lit on fire so maybe Vella won actually."

"Didn't she die?" Grimm said and sat up. "I think Thad won that battle, Roy." Grimm sat back and raised an eyebrow to Joy.

"Well for once I actually think you're right!" Roy laughed and stepped out the door.

Grimm leaned back and put his arms across the top of the long seat. He crossed his legs and winked. "I'm always right."

"Is that so?" Joy leaned forward and took another biscuit. Her hunger had caught up with her and had Grimm's eyes not been burning into her she would have tipped the entire contents of the tin into her mouth.

"You really are quite the beauty," Grimm said.

"I just killed your boss." Joy cocked her head to a side. "And all you can do is comment on that."

"I worked for Jane. She wasn't my boss. I'm my own boss. Top up?" Grimm popped the cork and held the bottle out in Joy's direction.

"Sure." She lifted her cup and watched the liquid tumble in.

"You mentioned that you have something better than those doubloons for me?" Grimm topped up his own glass and sank back into the seat.

Joy pulled out the button sized coin and displayed the piece of silver in her palm. "Recognize this?"

Grimm moved his face close to her hand. "Brothers and sisters of the white fox," he said.

Joy clasped her hand shut.

Grimm smiled. "I see where this is going but I don't know that it will get you much once word spreads of Jane's death. Let me have a closer look."

Joy pulled out a blade and held it up. "If you try anything."

"I don't think I'd be so stupid." Grimm raised his brows and stuck out his hand.

Joy dropped the coin into his palm.

"This is good for three favors. You see the little notches on the coin? Whoever carries out the favor scratches one out."

"That's what I was led to believe. I just don't understand what the person performing the favor gets out of it?" Joy asked and shrugged.

"Well, if you perform a favor you get to ask Jane for one in return. It has to be considered reasonable though. Could be to forgive a debt, whores for a week." Grimm smiled. "You've got to negotiate well but with Jane that's hard. Was hard." Grimm rubbed his thumb over the coin. "Ha! One time, I asked--"

"I don't want to hear it." Joy went to snatch the coin from his hand, but he clasped it shut. She lurched forward and grabbed him by his shirt collar and pulled him into her chest. She held her blade to his face. "The coin, Grimm."

He opened his hand. "Of course. I just wanted an excuse for you to get close to me."

Joy snatched the coin and shook it in her closed fist. She looked to the ceiling. "Can this still get me a favor or not?"

"Well, she's dead now isn't she?" Grimm re-arranged his shirt collar. "How many people know?"

Pirates of Nassau

"For now, me, you, Roy. It's only been a few hours," Joy said. It was a stretch of the truth but she wasn't bothered.

Grimm ran his hand through his slick black hair and folded his arms.

"You want the coin with two favors or the doubloons?" Joy asked.

"But there are three?"

"I need it back," Joy said.

Grimm narrowed his eyes. His eyebrows dropped and the corners of his mouth turned down in thought. "Give me the coin and I'll use it to get some favors from people before word gets around she's dead."

"Deal." Joy held out the coin for him to take. "If you give me this coin back and all the notches are ticked, I'll kill you."

Grimm took the coin and grinned. "Means I get to see you again though doesn't it."

Joy ignored his lecherous gaze. "The name, Grimm? That's why I'm here. Who was it?"

"Do you know of someone they call, The Boss?"

Joy clenched her fists by her side. "I do." She dug her fingernails into her palms. She should have stuck around and finished that fucker off.

"Well, he ships children off to Devils Cay to a man named, Seef. I don't know what exactly happens or why but that's where they end up."

"Seef," Joy repeated. "Does he ever come to Nassau?"

Grimm threw up his hands. "I hope not. From what I've heard he's... he's bad, Joy. I don't ever want any of this to come back to me." Grimm shook his head and readjusted his waistcoat.

"It won't." Joy looked back at Grimm. "Thanks for the biscuits." An icy calm came over her. She was one step closer.

"You're welcome." Grimm sprang to his feet.

Joy could tell her change in mood and sudden politeness unnerved him.

"I'll bring this back to you in a few days." He patted his front pocket where he placed the coin.

"You better. I'll let myself out."

Pirates of Nassau

Joy sped through the center. She couldn't wait to get home and see Raven. The streets looked exactly as they did before however they didn't carry the same feeling that they used to. After everything she'd been through, she wondered if anywhere ever would. As she reached the familiar streets of old town, she picked up her pace.

"Joy?" Raven stood outside of their house cleaning. "Joy!" She dropped her broom and ran towards her big sister.

Joy stretched out her arms and squeezed Raven tight. "Have you missed me?" Joy let go of her sister and smiled. She looked at the front of their house. "Looks like you've been busy. Probably didn't have a chance to notice I was gone!" She gave her little sister a light nudge.

"I missed you. You look exhausted, have you even eaten?" Raven said.

"Yes! But I've been saving myself for some of your home cooking." Joy smiled.

Raven frowned. Joy recognized the doubt in her eyes.

"Well, you best stick around for some then," Raven said.

"Joy! You're back!" A broad-shouldered muscular man stood by their front door and waved.

"Remember Tom? And his son Jim? They've been helping fix the place up." Raven said.

"Why?" Joy asked, confused.

Jim ran over, a grin spread across his sweet rosy cheeked face. "You helped us, we wanted to say thank you."

Joy swallowed the growing lump in her throat. She wasn't used to people being kind and, after what she'd been through, she found it hard to accept. "That's... so nice of you."

Raven grabbed Joy's arm and led her toward the house. "We have a door!"

Joy shook her head in astonishment. "Thank you."

"Fresh paint too," Tom said and opened the door. "Take a look inside."

Raven squeezed Joy's arm and buried her head into it. She sniffed loudly. "I think that jacket needs a wash!"

Joy laughed. "It certainly does."

Raven held out her hand.

Pirates of Nassau

Joy took off her jacket. "Hang on." She emptied the pockets into her vest. "All yours!"

"This is amazing. I can't believe it." Joy took off her hat and threw it in her room. After so many torturous weeks, it was a relief to be without all the heavy clothing. She walked back out with her hands clasped behind her back.

"What do you think?" Tom said and took off his hat, revealing a thick mop of hair.

"I think you deserve this." Joy thrust three doubloons into Tom's hand.

Tom gasped. "That's far too much. I can't accept this."

"What if I was to tell you I need a favor?" Joy smiled.

"Go on, Miss." Tom nodded.

"I've been offered a job and it's too good for me to refuse. Means I'll be gone a month or so though. I need you to check in on Raven if you could?"

"Of course! Are you sure you have to go though? She ain't half missed you," Tom said.

Jim came over and caught sight of the doubloons. His eyes grew wide and his mouth fell open a little.

"Those are for you and your dad." Joy smiled.

Jim looked over to Raven who stood by the door.

"Did I hear you say you have to go again?" Raven asked. Her voice quivered.

Joy hung her head and sighed. "This will be the last time. I promise." She walked over to Raven with her arms out. "I just want us to have a good life and this will mean we do." Joy brought Raven in close and held her tight. She could feel her body shake as she tried to stifle sobs. Raven pulled away.

"I'm sick of being on my own." She rubbed at her eyes.

Jim ran over and put his arm around Raven. "You're not though, you have us. Right, dad?"

"We'll check in on Raven for you. Make sure she's safe." Tom nodded. "Come Jim, let's leave them to it." The pair put away their tools and headed down the path back into town.

Pirates of Nassau

Joy reached for Raven's arm, but she shrugged it off and stormed inside. Joy caught up to her.

"Why?" Raven stomped her foot. "Why Joy?"

"I'm sorry but I think this is right for us." Joy hated lying to her. "We'll never have to worry again!" Joy turned and walked toward her bedroom. "I've something for you. Wait there."

"Fine." Raven dragged her feet and went into the kitchen.

Joy hated upsetting her sister like this. She'd already been through so much, but she couldn't live with herself knowing other children like Raven were being held at the mercy of that monster. She took out all the doubloons from her jacket and counted. She would keep two for herself and give the rest to Raven. Joy poked her head around the kitchen door. Raven sat with her head hung low and her hands clasped. The occasional tear dripped off her chin onto her skirt. It broke Joy's heart, but she had to go.

"Raven?"

Raven didn't look up. Joy sat next across from her. "Here's ten doubloons." She unloaded the golden coins onto the tiny kitchen table.

"What?" Raven covered her mouth with her hands. Her eyes lit up. "How?"

"It was the job."

"We're rich Joy!"

"Now can I have some of that home cooking? I've been dreaming of your chicken soup."

Raven sprang to her feet a ladled hot soup into a bowl. She beamed as she set it down on the table for Joy to enjoy.

Joy slurped the hot soup down. "This... I've missed this."

"Bread?" Raven tore off a wedge and handed it to Joy.

"Thank you." For the first time in a longtime a glimmer of happiness tickled Joy's heart.

"I still want you to stay." Raven sat back down. "Haven't we got enough now?"

"Like I said, this is the last job. It's on a different island, so I'll be gone a month or so but Tom and Jim will keep you company. They seem like good people." Joy tried to catch her sister's eye as she spooned in another mouthful of soup.

Pirates of Nassau

"They are. They've really fixed the place up." Raven held out her hand to Joy. "When will it ever be enough?"

Joy gave it a squeeze and ignored her sister's question. "I have to leave tonight. I know I've only just come home but next time, I'll be back for good."

Raven sighed. "Then I best finish cleaning your jacket."

Joy sat in her freshly painted kitchen savoring her soup. She looked at the stack of doubloons on the table. She was proud of how far she'd come, of what she'd survived, but her mission wasn't done yet. She had to find a way to Devils Cay and knew exactly who might be crazy enough to help her.

Captain Crow

Smudges of blood covered the once immaculate royal blue door of Vella's house. Crow led the way and kicked the door open. His men carried Vella and Popino behind him. Inside, those unharmed rushed about the reception area tending to those injured. Crow's eyes fixed on Georgia, the lip-ringed door-greeter, disheveled and bloodied but seemingly unharmed.

"Captain! We don't want no trouble." Georgia held up her hands.

"Neither do I; we've brought Vella."

Georgia's mouth fell open. "Miss V? But we lost her."

"She deserves a proper burial," Crow said. His men trailed in behind him. They placed Vella's body on the floor. His eyes shot down. He stared at her matted, muddied dreadlocked hair and pale face. His heart filled with sorrow. Vella's people ran to her side. Georgia didn't move. She stood shaking her head.

"I can't believe she's gone," Georgia said.

Isaac tumbled in through the door, with two of Crow's men carrying Popino.

"Popino?" Georgia rushed over.

"You know him?" Crow said.

"Every woman does," Isaac said under his breath. "Where can we put him?"

Pirates of Nassau

"Through here, follow me." Georgia led them to a large book-filled room with wood paneled walls.

Crow recognized it well, but he didn't let on.

"Lay him down by the window, draw the drapes," Georgia said. She put her hand to her mouth and shook her head. "Miss V wouldn't be happy having him here. He owed a lot."

"He's not all bad. I stole from him, otherwise he'd have paid her back," Isaac said and frantically nodded his head. "You have to help us Georgia, please?"

Georgia leant on a nearby desk and let out a huge breath. "He needs help. We have someone. I'll get one of the girls to find them." Georgia ran out of the door.

Crow turned around. His men had followed them in. "There's too many of us in here. Go help where you can. Don't go looting or try anything," Crow said to his men and gave a wry smile.

Underneath the tall window Isaac knelt by his friend's side. "You'll be fine Pino, might even have you a new lady friend."

Pino stirred.

"Pino? Can you hear me?" Isaac said.

"Check his head, boy, is he hot?" Crow said.

Isaac put his palm to Popino's forehead. "Not really."

"He might just pull through," Crow said.

Georgia came back in the room with an older silver-haired woman by her side.

"This is Grace, she's our healer. She'll fix him," Georgia said.

Grace hurried past them with a basket of cloths and potions in hand.

"Thank you! Please, if the cook is here, tell them I'm sorry. We just want to make things right. Pino and I both do," Isaac said.

Crow grabbed Isaac by the arm and pulled him aside. "What did you do to the cook?" Crow said.

Georgia frowned and crossed her arms.

"Nothing!" Isaac smiled.

"It seems I'm in charge now, Captain. Miss V said if she were to die in battle, then all command goes to me." Georgia dug her hand into her jacket and retrieved a piece of tough parchment. "She signed it before we attacked." Georgia thrust the parchment toward Crow. "I know about you two, you don't have to pretend."

Crow scratched at his beard and remained silent. He took the parchment and skimmed over the scrawled text, then handed it back to Georgia. Crow was at a loss for words. He'd lost everyone he ever loved in such a short space of time. A knock on the door interrupted them. He felt a moment of relief at the interruption. He didn't want people to think him weak. He sure as hell wasn't, but he was still human.

Georgia rushed to the door. "Come. Let's leave Grace to work her magic."

Crow and Isaac left Popino with Grace. A scrawny, grubby looking man stood in the reception area.

"I recognize you! I've seen you about the tavern. Otis isn't it?" Isaac said.

The man stared through him. "I have a message for you." Otis held out a piece of paper to Crow. "From Thad."

"What if I don't want it?" Crow said and crossed his arms.

"I'll leave it anyway," Otis said.

"Fine!" Crow snatched the paper.

Otis looked side to side then walked away, avoiding the bodies. He ran out the door.

Crow unfolded the paper and scanned the words. He smiled. "Whoops!"

"What's it say?" Isaac asked, his eyes eager.

Crow read aloud. "You killed my son and now I'm going to kill you. You can try to run but there's no escaping what's coming to you -- Thad, or as you may now know me, Molly."

"Molly?" Crow looked up and confused. "I've killed a lot of late. I don't even know who her son is at this point."

"Molly's Thad?" Isaac said and covered his mouth. "But I've played chess with her."

"Makes a bit more sense why she had Nelson. Do you think that prick Ives knew?" Crow said.

"He could have been an inside man," Georgia replied. "Either way, we'll stand with you Captain."

Pirates of Nassau

"Thank you, Georgia." Crow fumbled with the paper and considered who Molly's son might be.

Isaac hadn't moved. His mouth fell open so wide that his jaw could have hit the floor.

"You'll catch flies, boy," Crow said.

"I just can't believe it," Isaac replied. He reached into his pocket. "These cards will haunt me. Does Thad have a symbol?"

"Dog, maybe?" Crow replied. The boy seemed more shocked than he expected. Then again not much surprised Crow. He'd been around long enough to know better and he certainly wasn't going to be intimidated by threats, even if they did come from Thad.

Isaac pointed to one of the cards and muttered to himself.

A loud knock on the front door interrupted. "I'm not armed," a muffled voice said. The door pushed open an inch. "Hello? I'm looking for Isaac Carver?"

"Joy! It's okay, I know her." Isaac stumbled over the bodies towards the front door. He pulled it open and hugged the beautiful woman tight. "Are you okay? Why are you here?"

"I can't believe I'm saying this, but it's good to see you." She looked over at Crow.

He paused and stared at her soft face, dumbstruck by her beauty. Besides, he didn't think the boy had any friends. Let alone one that would dare come and find him here. "Boy! You going to introduce your friend?"

"Joy Lafitte everybody," Isaac said and held out his arm toward her.

Crow cleared his throat.

"And this is Captain Crow," Isaac said.

"A pleasure to meet you miss," Crow grabbed her by the hand and bent down to kiss it. She slipped out of his grasp and extended her hand for a shake.

"I've seen you around. You and your man Nelson," Joy said.

Isaac shook his head.

"What?" Joy said and looked at Isaac.

"He's dead," Isaac mouthed.

"Oh, I'm sorry Captain. I didn't know. Seems a lot are," Joy said and looked around.

"Call me, Crow. It's a pleasure to meet you, Joy."

Joy gave Isaac a nudge. "You never mentioned you were friends with a famous Captain."

Crow smiled and puffed out his chest a little. "Well, I wouldn't say we're friends." He scratched at his beard and laughed. He looked to Isaac who seemed hurt by the comment. "Oh, I'm kidding. We're the best of friends now, aren't we boy?" He put his arm around Isaac and pulled him in.

"You stink." Isaac pushed Crow away and blocked his nose. "Yeah, we're friends." Isaac rolled his eyes and shook his head. "Popino's here. I know you and him never got along but--"

"Ha! You and me both." Crow winked.

Isaac glared. "He's been shot. His little girls gone too," Isaac said.

"I know. Well, about Rose, I think it's the same person that took Raven," Joy said.

"What? How do you? Never mind. Who are they?" Isaac said.

"There's two of them. One called, Seef lives in Devil's Cay, then this other man called The Boss ships them to him. That's where Rose will be."

"Devil's Cay!" Isaac said and slapped Crow on the shoulder. "Hear that? Same place the treasure is buried."

Crow stroked at his beard. "Aha."

"We know where the treasure is Joy," Isaac said his eyes wide with excitement. "Finally!" Isaac scratched the back of his neck.

Crow hadn't seen him like this before. He looked almost bashful.

"I mean I actually found out a while ago but then Crow's shack exploded, Relocke arrested me, Johnny broke me out then held me captive. Then there was the whole war of course..." Isaac trailed off.

"A lot's happened, miss," Crow added.

"Looks like we're all going to Devil's Cay then." Joy turned to Crow and smiled.

"Now hold up there miss, I don't know if we'll have room, there's a full crew."

Joy took out her blade. "I can make room if I need to."

Crow belted out a laugh so loud it almost shook the room. "You can have his place!"

Pirates of Nassau

He pointed to Isaac and wiped a tear from his eye. "Have you sailed before?"

"I'm sure you can teach me," Joy replied.

"Can you lot get out of here? Go be with Popino," Georgia held out her arms and ushered them out. "He's resting."

Isaac grinned from ear to ear and grabbed Georgia's waist. "Resting? So he's okay?"

Georgia nodded.

"Thank you!" Isaac pulled Georgia toward him and threw his arms around her.

They walked into the book-filled room. Popino lay underneath the window, resting.

"Pino!" Isaac crept over.

"Leave him be. He's not to be disturbed," Grace said and left the room with bandages and pots of ointment in hand.

"Sorry!" Isaac whispered.

Crow took a seat at the writing desk. Joy and Isaac joined him.

"Is your ship ready?" Joy asked.

"Well..." Crow patted down his jacket. He stuck his hand in his pockets. "It um needs a bit of work but I admire your enthusiasm."

"How much?" Joy pressed.

"Sixty doubloons worth," Crow rushed the words out.

"Sixty!" Isaac said. His eyes grew wide.

Crow scratched at his beard. He looked down. It had grown considerably and there was more gray than he last remembered. "I've got that ones doubloons, somewhere." He nodded in Popino's direction.

"What do you mean, somewhere?" Isaac said.

"Hang on!" Crow untied his pants.

"Okay." Joy looked away.

"I've a hole in my pocket, so I tied it inside," Crow said and retrieved a pouch full of coins.

Isaac shook his head.

Crow tied his pants back up and looked at Joy. "I like your hat."

"I like your jacket," Joy said.

"Well, we've two problems. There's no ship without those doubloons, plus the waters at Devil's Cay are treacherous. Only three people have ever made it there and back alive." Crow held out his hand and counted. "Thad, some man named Leon and..." Crow tapped the table.

"Slim!" Crow and Joy said in unison.

"How do you know him?" Crow asked.

"We're from the same part of town." Joy straightened up her jacket. "I can go talk to him if you like. He's always happy to see me."

"Already proving to be more useful than the boy, might have you take his place after all." Crow laughed. "Now we just need the doubloons."

"Oh, and don't forget that Thad is going to hunt you down and kill you," Isaac said and folded his arms.

"Do you know that Thad is actually Molly?" Joy said.

"Yes!" Crow and Isaac replied in unison.

"Sounds like you need a Master Strategist," Georgia walked in with Grace. The healer scurried over to Popino and changed the cloth on his head.

"I'll get you the map Isaac," Georgia said and shot him a wink as she left.

Crow noticed Joy's eyes narrow at the gesture.

"We have company!" Georgia yelled and came running back in. "Jane's people are outside! Prepare your weapons!"

"I didn't think any had survived?" Crow said and pulled out his pistol.

Crow followed Georgia and crept into the reception area. He ran to the front window and peeled back the drape. "They're waving a piece of white cloth. I think they're here to surrender."

"It's probably a trick," Georgia said.

"They don't look armed," Crow replied. He counted a group of twenty or so people. They stood at the front door with their hands up. "Brave coming here... or stupid."

Georgia flung the door open and pointed her rifle. Several women rushed to her side wielding weapons.

Pirates of Nassau

"We don't want trouble. We want to join you," a slight dark-haired man said.

"Not interested. We don't take men," Georgia said.

"I'll take 'em," Crow said and stepped away from the window. "Any of you sailed before?"

"No, but we can learn," the dark-haired man nodded.

"Then, I'll take the women if you go with him," Georgia said.

The crew of mercenaries nodded.

"Try anything and I'll skin you alive," Crow said and followed it with a hearty laugh. He waved them in and walked back through the reception. "Now, how do we get sixty doubloons." He scratched at his head and thought of Nelson. What would he do?

Molly Weaver

"What did he say?" Molly looked up from her workspace for a moment. She had been experimenting for days. It kept her mind busy until she could have her day with him. With Crow.

"He wasn't going to take it, the note," Otis said.

"What?" Molly picked up a bottle and hurled the brown glass at the wall. The pieces shattered and scattered across the floor. "That coward! He's not going to know what's hit him by the time I've finished." She picked up a dagger she used to crush up powder and stabbed the point into the desk. "I've had enough of waiting." She grabbed her chair and smashed the wooden frame into the wall over and over. The legs splintered and the seat fell to the ground. Her leg still ached every time her rage surged. She'd tried her best to let the wound heal but it was hard to keep her anger under control. She'd survived that hellhole of a prison only to find Daniel gone. Dead. She could never make things right now. Crow's face haunted her. She threw down the remnants of the chair and stormed out of her room. "Otis!"

"Yes ma'am, coming." Otis hurried out of the room after her.

Molly walked towards the steep stone steps. The bottom layer of her infamous castle was where she spent most of her time. She was typically alone but those unlucky enough to join her down here didn't usually come out alive. Not only was it the perfect place to torture but also to experiment with explosives or anything else that came to mind.

Pirates of Nassau

As Molly climbed the steps she admired the thick stone. This place was solid and sturdy just like her. The castle stood at the tallest point of Nassau, surrounded by a moat of water. For so long nobody had known she was the one behind this whole operation. People respected her as Molly, but they never knew she was capable of this. Thad was the most feared man in Nassau and he didn't even exist. A glimmer of satisfaction brought a wry smile to her face. Her plan to gain Vella's trust then drive her to attack Jane had taken years but she'd finally done it. Though any feelings of victory were short-lived when she thought of Daniel. All she ever wanted was him back in her life but Crow had taken that from her. Vengeance wouldn't bring him back but it sure would help make her feel better. And once Crow was taken care of she would step out from the shadows and claim Nassau as she so rightfully deserved.

She headed down the long corridor. Otis trod softly behind.

"Ma'am?"

"Yes, Otis."

"I don't fully understand some things. A few of us don't actually," his voice wavered as he spoke. He quickened his pace to keep up with Molly's huge strides. Even with an injured leg they were still substantial.

"And why do you need to?" She stopped dead in her tracks and turned to face him. He almost smacked into her but stopped just short. "I don't think you're in a position to query my motives. Especially when you withheld information."

"I didn't, I swear, I just never made the connection that he was your... your son." Otis stared up at her.

Molly shook her head and tried to keep her temper in check. Otis had been nothing but loyal for so many years. He'd slipped up on this one, but she couldn't ignore everything else he'd done for her. He was one of the very few she trusted. "What is it you want to know?"

"Why..." He shifted awkwardly and held onto his arm, "why did you have us slaughter everyone at the Milky Way? Otis scrunched up his face.

"It had to be done. Drove Vella to finally attack Jane didn't it?" Molly said.

Pirates of Nassau

Otis scratched as his head. "But we liked that place?"

"Go to the Silky Swallow instead." Molly shrugged. "I don't expect you to understand my reasons but I expect you not to question them." Molly turned and continued walking. "Besides, we didn't kill them all now, did we?"

"I guess," Otis mumbled and shuffled behind.

"Ma'am!" A strong looking dark-haired man walked toward Molly and Otis.

"Patrick." She gave a nod of acknowledgment.

"The perimeter's been lined with that... that clam thing you made," Patrick said.

"You mean the, Clam Bam, Patrick?"

"The name, it's--"

"It's a clam and it makes a loud bam!" Molly smacked her hands together.

Otis and Patrick flinched.

"I'd like to see you come up with something better." Molly crossed her arms and widened her stance.

"Of course, I couldn't." Patrick looked to the floor.

"How's the concoction going? The liquid courage. Are the men ready for anything?" Molly asked.

"Seem to be. Few hurled their guts up but that's probably the amount they drank." Patrick laughed.

"To be expected. Have them ready soon would you, we don't want to give Crow time to plan anything." Molly nodded and proceeded down the corridor. She passed through a tall archway and walked into the dining hall. Rows of dark wooden tables and benches filled the long room. Wrought iron candelabras hung from the ceiling and illuminated the huge space.

"Otis, eat something. I'll call you over when you're needed."

He bowed his head and ran over to where the cook served up the hot meats of the day.

Molly's eyes scanned the room for Arnaud. He wouldn't be hard to spot since he usually wore such unique attire. Molly walked over to the far corner where a slight man sat with his feet kicked up on a bench. "You stand out a mile off," Molly said and took a seat opposite him. He swung his legs down and faced Molly. He wore a bright blue hat with a neckerchief to match and a pale blue almost gray, linen shirt with the arms rolled up.

"I assume that is because I'm impeccably dressed," he spoke with a thick French accent.

"This is new?" Molly pointed to a glinting gold locket around his neck.

He rubbed at the circular gold piece with his thumb and forefinger. "Bonne chance," he replied and looked down at the sketch he was working on.

Arnaud was quick-witted, astute and an exceptional artist. These skills not only made him the most valuable informant in Nassau but also the most expensive.

Molly clasped her hands together and leaned on the table. "Tell me Arnaud, do you know of a man they call, The Boss?"

"Describe him to me," Arnaud said and pushed his sketchbook aside.

Molly cast her mind back to the cell. "Missing front tooth, weathered--"

"That is everybody in Nassau," Arnaud said.

Molly gave a glimmer of a smile. "True. His attire is actually quite distinct. Dresses head-to-toe in black and red. Heavy captain's jacket with an unusual gold pin on the lapel."

"A gold serpent?" Arnaud said.

"Could be?" Molly replied.

He grabbed his sketchbook and thumbed through the pages. "Ah." He stopped and turned the book to face Molly.

She cast her eyes over a detailed sketch of three mean-faced men. "That's him." Molly pointed then clenched her fists.

"They're known as, The Serpents of Death," Arnaud said.

Molly's eyes grew wide. She'd never heard anything about them. "Go on." Molly felt a rush of excitement. She had hoped Arnaud would have the information she needed.

"They've been around for years but don't stay in Nassau for long."

"Where do they go?"

"I don't know. Though I'd be happy to investigate...find out some more for you."

"I thought you'd have a little more on them considering your detailed sketch?" Molly suspected he was holding something back.

"I draw anything of interest. It doesn't mean I have all the information," Arnaud replied.

Molly nodded and looked over her shoulder. "Otis!" Molly yelled and waved in his direction. He didn't flinch and kept spooning in his stew. Molly rubbed her hand against her forehead. "Why must I..." Molly stood up. She cast a long shadow that engulfed him. He nodded and put down his spoon.

"You want me?" Otis said.

Molly nodded and beckoned him over with her finger. He grabbed his satchel and hurried over. "Arnaud will explain more but I need you to work together on this, find out everything you can."

"Together? Okay ma'am," Otis replied.

"Yes. It's of the utmost importance. I need to know their every move." She looked at Arnaud. "You will of course be paid handsomely for your troubles."

"Bien sûr." Arnaud gave a tip of his hat and tucked his sketchbook under his arm. He motioned to the door with his head and Otis followed, leaving Molly alone with her thoughts as vengeance boiled in her heart.

Popino Beltrame

"Now, how do we get sixty doubloons." Popino heard a gruff voice say followed by loud footsteps. He told himself to open his eyes, but they wouldn't cooperate. He tried to move but nothing responded. He lay for what felt like an eternity unable to speak, listening to the chatter of voices. He could have sworn he heard Isaac as he drifted back off to sleep.

He awoke. It seemed like only moments later, but this time his body felt different, more responsive. He focused on moving his hand and gave a small wave, hoping someone would notice.

"I need rum to strategize!"

Popino recognized the chirpy tone. "Isaac?" he said softly and waved again.

"He's coming round, boy," the gruff voice said.

"Pino?" Isaac came hurtling over. He knelt by his side and gave his arm a squeeze. "You're alive!"

Popino winced at his touch. Any movement right now sent throbbing waves of pain through his entire body.

"Get him some water or something."

The voice sounded like Joy's. Popino started to wonder if he was dreaming.

Pirates of Nassau

"Where am I?" He stared up at Isaac. His face looked more rugged than ever.

"We're at Vella's place," Isaac said.

Popino's eyes grew wide. Was he in danger?

"It's okay, she's dead," Isaac whispered.

Popino let his eyes fall shut again. "Rose?" he asked.

"She's definitely not here. Joy thinks she might be in Devil's Cay," Isaac said.

Popino scrunched his eyes tight. He just wanted this nightmare to end. "Did..." He took a breath in and was met with a deep stabbing pain in his side. "Did we win?"

"Win what? The battle? Nobody really won. Most are dead," Isaac said.

Popino touched his bandaged side.

"You got shot, but lucky for you the ball seems to have passed right through." Isaac nodded.

"It hurts. A lot," Popino said and tried to sit up. Searing pain blazed at his side. "Think I'll just lay here," he said, his voice faint.

The man with the gruff voice cast a shadow over him. "Remember me?"

Popino stared up at the crinkled face. He had a long thick salt and pepper beard and a well-worn black captain's jacket. Popino shook his head.

"This is Captain Crow, Pino. Remember? I told you about him." Isaac nodded and shot Popino a wink.

"The map. Sorry," Popino muttered.

"Hmm." Crow grunted as he walked away.

A strong looking woman with a spiral of gray beaded dreads strode into the room. Isaac moved aside, and she took his place at Popino's side. She tipped a tumbler of liquid into his mouth. The bitter aftertaste wasn't pleasant, but he was grateful to have some fluid back in his body.

"You shouldn't have left Roy's!" Joy walked into view and smiled. "I was planning on coming back you know."

Pirates of Nassau

He nodded. The gray-haired woman gave a tip of her head and disappeared. He cleared his throat. "I'm confused. How do you know she's in Devil's Cay? Did Vella send Rose there?" Popino asked.

Joy shook her head. "It wasn't Vella."

"The note though?" Popino said, his voice strained as a wave of pain surged through him.

"Must have been fake. She's been kidnapped by the same people that took Raven." Joy's eyes fixed on the floor. "I tried to find her, but I think they'd already taken her."

Popino shut his eyes. "Do we know who they are?"

"We do, and I'm going to hunt them down myself." Joy held a clenched fist to her mouth. "They call one, The Boss. He's in charge here in Nassau but works for a man named Seef."

Popino nodded and opened his eyes. He stared at Joy's beautiful soft face. Her delicate skin reminded him of Rose. His poor girl would be scared out of her mind...He wanted to slit their throats. Carve out their hearts. Popino swallowed hard. "So, nothing to do with Vella?"

"I really don't think so. Rest anyway. You need to get better. Won't survive the journey to Devils Cay otherwise." Joy gave him a smile and walked away.

Crow scowled. "Who said he could come? Come on, boy, we've planning to do." Crow sat at a writing desk and jiggled a map at Isaac. "Can't let Thad get to us first." Crow frowned and looked to the floor. "She's the reason Nelson's dead." Crow flexed his hand and made a tight fist. Popino could tell it took everything in him not to smash it into the table.

Popino's mind cast back to the battle and what that strange man had said. "You know... someone told me that Molly is Thad?" Popino said in a faint whisper.

Isaac nodded. "Yes! I still can't believe it! Now, where is that rum?"

The lip-ringed door-greeter walked in with a bottle in hand. "Here you go!" She handed the bottle to Isaac who took a seat next to Crow. "Oh hello," she said and walked over to Popino. She knelt at his bedside. "Glad to see you're awake." She took the cloth from his head. "I'll have Grace get you another." She placed her hand on his.

"Thank you. Thank you for this." Popino flashed a smile.

"You're welcome," she said and put her mouth to his ear. "I know about Thomas."

Popino's eyes grew wide. He shook his head. "Who?"

"At the Boucher house --Thomas was Vella's son," Georgia whispered and squeezed his hand. "But don't worry, your secret's safe with me. I'll figure out repayment." Her hand wandered down to his crotch.

Popino coughed. "Yes, thank you, okay. Thank you."

"I'll have Grace come with that cloth." She shot him a wink and rose to her feet.

Popino lay still and stared at the beige ceiling in horror. He certainly hadn't forgotten what had happened with Eva and Lucien, but it had been pushed to the back of his mind when Rose was taken. He wondered how many people knew about the Boucher incident? He'd surely be hanged for their murders.

"What's this?" Crow waved something in his hand and interrupted Popino's racing thoughts.

"Put it back on the map. It's for planning. Vella, Jane, Thad, they all have one," Isaac said and snatched the small carved wooden wolf from Crow's hand. "The wolf represents Vella's people."

"You can take Jane's away," Joy said and took a seat at the table. "She's dead." Joy grabbed the wooden fox figure.

"Dead?" Popino raised his head.

"Can I keep this actually?" Joy waved the fox at Crow and Isaac. They nodded in response.

Popino put his head back down on the makeshift pillow and closed his eyes. For the first time in a long time a wave of relief washed over him. If Jane was dead then he didn't need to pay her, and with Vella out of the picture too there was no one left that he owed coin to. Georgia seemed to want something else from him and he was happy to oblige. Could he finally be debt free after all these years? It didn't bring Rose back but it would help them once he found her... eventually. He'd need to deal with the Boucher incident though. He hoped it really was just a secret.

Isaac swigged from the rum bottle. "I don't know how to even get close to that giant castle. It's surrounded by water."

Pirates of Nassau

Crow scratched at his beard. "Hmm. What about the doubloons? I need sixty to fix Black Beauty." His eyes twinkled as he spoke.

"Is that your ship's name? I can't wait to see her. Is she like The Fancy?" Isaac asked.

"Better, boy. You just wait," Crow replied.

"I have some." Popino waved his hand.

"Ships?" Crow said and let out a raucous laugh.

"Doubloons," Popino said.

Crow scratched at his beard. "So do I. Well, they're yours actually." He walked toward Popino and stood over him. He pulled out the pouch and tossed it on the floor. "Thirty, I believe. The boy said I was to give them back to you."

"How about you keep them as payment. I need to come to Devil's Cay, but I won't be much use until this fully heals." Popino looked down at his side. "I have more too." He patted his belt. "I took them from Vella."

"Ever the thief!" Crow looked around to check if Vella's people were around. "It's our secret, okay?" His eyes burned into him.

"Yes, of course. And I can sail with you?" Popino tried to sit up. He closed his eyes tight as pain shot through him.

"Not sure how much sailing you can do but sure. It's a deal. Now don't move kid, I'll untie that pouch." Crow reached over and fiddled with Popino's belt. Popino turned his head to the side and looked away, hoping that the Captain would just untie the pouch and not slit his throat. "Thank you for keeping your word. Isaac told me you would."

"I always do." Crow shook the pouch and grinned. "Black Beauty will be back on the water before we know it. Now, who's going to see Woodman Jack?" Crow asked and looked at Joy.

Joy scrunched up her face. "Fine!"

"You have certain assets he appreciates. Might help us get a better price. Besides, it seems you can handle yourself," Crow said.

"Yeah, yeah." Joy rolled her eyes. "I'll go see Slim, then Woodman Jack. But first I need a word with you, in private." Joy pointed at Isaac.

Isaac pointed at himself and raised his eyebrows.

"Lucky!" Popino winked and smiled.

Pirates of Nassau

Joy and Isaac walked out leaving Crow and Popino alone.

Popino lay there and thought of Rose. He tried not to panic himself, but he couldn't help it. She'd be so frightened. If he hadn't borrowed so much. If he hadn't gone to the brothel that day, he wouldn't be in this mess. The thoughts played over and over in his head. The guilt gnawed at his gut. Occasional grunts came from Crow's direction.

"Can I help?" Popino asked.

"Any good with strategy? Crow said.

Popino shook his head. "Good with a pistol though."

"Well, that will come in handy later. Where's the boy? They've been gone a while."

Popino smiled. "You know they're probably just..."

Isaac and Joy strode in through the door smiling.

Joy snatched up the pouches of doubloons and attached them to her belt. "I'll be off then. You three better have a plan for Thad by the time I return," she said as she walked out the door.

"Doubt it." Crow grumbled once more.

Nobody had moved from the room in hours. Isaac occasionally strode around stroking at his chin and demanding more rum. Crow sat scratching his beard, grunting. And Popino lay in his makeshift bed, trying his best to rest.

"Why does Thad want you dead anyway?" Popino asked. He sat up a little and this time the pain was manageable. He propped himself against the wall underneath the window.

"Killed her son apparently." Crow shrugged.

"Thunder?" Popino cocked his head to the side. "Big guy, arms as big as my head?"

Crow looked up and narrowed his eyes in thought. "Is that who it was. He killed Vella so..."

Popino kept quiet. Thunder had done him a favor, but he didn't think Crow would appreciate hearing that.

"That's it!" Isaac yelled. He stopped pacing and stood frozen to the spot.

"Yes, yes, yes!" He ran over to the map. "Joy told me a story while we were--"

59

"I hope she waited for you to finish." Popino slapped at his thigh and laughed.

Isaac shot him a look of disapproval followed by a smile. "I've got it. I know how to get to Thad."

Joy Lafitte

"Slim! There you are!"

"Miss Joy! It's been far too long since I laid my eyes on your loveliness." Slim limped towards her. He was a short scrawny man who looked underfed and despite the glorious Nassau weather, like he had never seen the sun. "To what do I owe the pleasure?" He gave a small bow.

Joy peered down the alleyway where Slim crouched beneath a window. "I need your help. But first, what are you doing here?"

"I need to break in you see. There's something that these men have that I want." He placed his hand on his chest.

Joy crept toward him and kept low. He pointed up to the window and grinned. Joy stole a glance inside the wooden hut. Three brutish men stood with their heads down, gathered around a table assembling weapons. She quickly ducked "What is this place?"

"Thad's weapon store." Slim nodded, his eyes filled with mischief.

"Well, what you want better be worth it." Joy crouched and kept out of sight.

"Oh, it is Miss Joy." Slim rubbed his hands together and grinned. "Look again and you'll see something on the table to the right."

Joy raised her head and looked to the right. "There's a big greenish ball, or is that thing a fruit?"

"Melon!" Slim said and licked his lips.

Pirates of Nassau

Joy shrugged, "I don't know it."

"It's rare in these parts but I've had a taste before. It's too good to miss." Slim smiled. "If you help me, I'll split it with you."

Joy thought about Slim's proposition. She could care less about tasting this thing, but she did need his help. And if she needed to battle these three brutes for that, then she would. "If I do it, will you help me with my request?"

Slim's eyes widened with enthusiasm. "What is it?"

"I need you to navigate a crew of us to Devil's Cay," Joy said.

Slim threw his arms in the air. "Of course! You know my brother's still there, Miss Joy?"

"I didn't, but I know you're one of few to make it there and back alive."

"One of three people!" Slim held his finger in the air. "But first we must have the melon. That's my one and only condition."

Joy rolled her eyes. "You're going to risk it all for that melon?"

"You haven't tasted it! Plus, with your help there's no risk, Miss Joy. I just need you to provide the distraction." He looked her up and down. "Any man is distracted by you."

Joy let her jacket fall open and pulled down her top. "They're distracted by these. Ha! Let's make our way to the door. Then I'll go ahead and pretend to be lost." Joy led the way. She walked around the corner and assessed the door. The well-worn wood didn't look like it would be hard to kick down, and it had no lock. She strode over and pushed the door open. To her surprise it swung back and she walked in with her hands on her hips. She stuck out her chest and gave her most charming smile. The men looked up startled. "Sorry boys, I think I'm lost. Can you help?"

"Oi! You're not meant to be in here," the tallest of the three said and placed a box on the ground. "This is private property."

The other two men wiped their dirty hands on rags in unison and leered at Joy.

"I know, but I'm lost and I thought you could help." Joy raised her eyebrows. She wasn't scared but she hoped Slim would step in soon. She needed to get to Woodman Jack's before sundown.

Pirates of Nassau

"How'd you find us in here? Who sent you?" the tall man asked and walked towards her. The other two stood behind him and folded their arms. She was about to reply and tell them they weren't as discreet as they thought they were when blood burst from their temples and they each dropped to the floor. Joy recoiled as some splattered onto her face.

Slim laughed. "That was much easier with you here!"

Joy turned to Slim. Her mouth fell open. "How did you...How did you get all three at once? I've never seen that before."

"It's my new rifle." He held up a long gun and unscrewed the barrel. "It's very powerful. It comes apart so you can carry it, see?" He took the barrel and shoved the metal tube down his pant leg. He smiled at his handiwork and attached the other part of the gun to his hip. "Plus, they were lined up in a row nicely. Now, where is that sweet fruit?"

"I didn't think you would kill them... for some melon?" Joy wiped the blood from her face with a nearby rag. Slim busied himself cutting the melon open with a thick carving knife.

"How far does that thing shoot?"

"Well, if you're good and take the wind into account. Very far. Made it myself I did," he said with pride and handed a piece of the juicy fruit to Joy.

She sniffed at the hunk of thick-skinned fruit and took a bite. "Do I eat these seeds?" she asked with her mouthful. The sweet soft flesh burst in her mouth.

"Spit 'em out. We should save some though, try plant our own." Slim's eyes went wide with glee as he sunk his teeth into the ripe flesh.

"This is good. Though not sure we should have killed three men for it," Joy said in between a mouthful.

"I'd say it's worth the price." Slim discarded the skin and sliced another piece. "So, who's heading the crew to Devil's Cay?"

"Captain Crow," Joy replied.

Slim grinned and rubbed his hands.

Pirates of Nassau

"I'm about to go see Woodman Jack to get the ship fixed. We should be ready to go soon," Joy said.

"I'll meet you later then. I'll go find Crow... and Nelson." Slim grabbed the remainder of the melon and limped out of the building.

"Just Crow, Nelson's dead. Oh, and they're at Vella's," Joy said.

"Nelson's dead? They're at Vella's?" He looked to the floor and shook his head. "If you say so Miss Joy. I'll be seeing you."

"Bye, Slim."

Joy headed for the old wood yard.

"Well, if it isn't the delightful Miss Lafitte," Grimm said. He stood next to Woodman Jack with his arms folded, staring at a broken ship hull. Woodman Jack was most definitely the bushiest man she had ever seen; a thick layer of white hair covered every inch of him. He wore a scruffy black shirt with rolled up sleeves and leant on an axe.

"What are you doing here?" Joy asked.

"I could ask you the same question," Grimm said.

"Maybe she's come to see me." Woodman Jack gave Grimm a nudge and leered at Joy for an uncomfortably long time.

"I certainly have." She stood with her hands on her hips and let her jacket fall open.

Woodman Jack didn't take his eyes off her. He stroked at his beard as he gazed at her chest.

Grimm noticed Woodman Jack's longing stare and shook his head. "Glad I bumped into you. I believe this is yours." Grimm twirled the button-sized coin in the air and caught it with ease. Joy held out her hand, unimpressed. He dropped the silver piece into her outstretched palm and attempted a smile.

"Thanks. Dare I asked what favor you called in?" Joy smirked.

"You don't want to know." Grimm winked. "Anyway, I best be heading off. Thank you, Jack, I'll let you know." Grimm walked away leaving Joy alone to negotiate.

Woodman Jack strode over to the broken ship hull and stroked at the wood. "She's a fine one." He turned to Joy and stared. "Just like you."

"We've business to discuss."

"Maybe a bit of fun first?"

Pirates of Nassau

It took everything in Joy not to storm over there and press a blade to his neck. "I need you to fix Black Beauty," Joy said and ignored his vulgarity.

"You can't afford it. Though I'm sure we could come to some arrangement."

Joy took out the sacks of doubloons and tossed them in front of him. "Check the bags, should be sixty."

His eyes grew wide with surprise. He threw down his axe and greedily snatched the sacks from the ground. Joy eyed the yard as Jack engrossed himself in counting. Dozens of battered and broken ship parts lay scattered as far as the eye could see. Some looked to be more barnacle than wood at this point and others merely looked damaged from battle.

"You've got enough coin," Jack said and offloaded the sacks into his own.

"I know." Joy smiled though it pained her.

"Tell Crow it'll take a week or two."

"Can it be done any quicker?"

"Well, that depends," Jack leered at her chest once more.

"I'll come back and visit each day?" Joy said.

"I might take my time then." He shot her a wink which made her skin crawl.

She marched over and whipped out one of her small blades. "Jack! If you do, I'll poke you with one of these!" She held the blade under his chin.

Jack leaned his head back. "It's worth it to feel you press up against me." He let out a longing sigh.

She grabbed his collar. "Don't. Push. It!" she said through gritted teeth.

"Fine, I'll have it done as soon as I can."

She released her grip and watched in disbelief as he sniffed at the part of his shirt she had touched. Joy rolled her eyes as she walked away. She loathed his lecherous behavior but he knew ships and that was all that mattered right now.

Joy fanned herself with her jacket as she made her way through the streets of town back to Vella's. The sun was still blazing hot despite the time of day. Out the corner of her eye she saw a man that looked exactly like Isaac, rush by. She'd recognize that handsome face anywhere, though she didn't like to admit it. "Isaac!" Joy yelled and ran after him.

He turned and glanced over his shoulder. "Oh Joy! It's just you. Thank goodness. I mean not just you. You know what I mean." He shrugged and looked a little bashful.

"What's in the bag? Shouldn't you be strategizing at Vella's?"

He shook his head. "I've got it! You gave me the idea."

Joy threw her hands up, confused.

"The story you told me about Jane's camp during the trial with Thunder, y'know? I'll explain, follow me. We need to attack Thad... before she gets to us!"

Molly Weaver

"I bring news." Arnaud smiled. He tipped his striking bright blue hat as he took a seat opposite Molly in the main hall.

Raucous chatter filled the room. Men sat drinking and cleaning their weapons, ready for battle. Otis perched on the bench next to Molly twiddling with the fastening on his satchel.

Arnaud flipped open his sketchbook. "See this?" He pointed to two ships side by side. "This smaller ship is the Fancy. You know it right?"

"Of course, but it's not small, it's one of the biggest to dock here. It hasn't moved in a long time," Molly said.

Arnaud nodded. "Yes, but this ship makes it look small." He pointed to the much larger vessel. "It's an old slave ship which now belongs to, The Serpents of Death."

Molly stared at the brass chunks which sat on the table before her; two custom-made pieces built to slot onto her knuckles. She'd never used them before, but they were sure to make for one hell of a fight. Her brows dipped and she pressed her lips together. "If it's so big then why haven't I seen it?"

"Exactly! Doesn't make sense, but that's because it never docks here. They keep this ship at a nearby island and take a much smaller one here which they keep in the backwaters."

Molly let out a huge sigh and tapped her finger on the tabletop.

Pirates of Nassau

Arnaud tipped his head. "It seems, The Boss had purposely stayed away from Nassau. Left the island to you, Vella and Jane but now..." Arnaud snapped his book shut.

"What does he want? The island?" Molly clenched her shaking fist. Arnaud nodded.

She banged her fist on the table. "I've waited too long and sacrificed too much to let anyone take it from me!" She tried to keep her voice low but it was difficult. She had spent years slowly weakening Vella and her people. Years of hiding in the shadows. This was her time and no man was about to take that away from her.

"Apparently they live in Devils Cay but come here for trade." Arnaud averted his gaze. "They take children from here."

Molly kept quiet and cracked her knuckles. A storm brewed inside of her. She hated everything about these 'Serpents'.

"Not many make it there and back alive, but they seem to have found a way around that." Arnaud shrugged. "I'm sure none of this will stop you getting what you want though." He smiled though it seemed forced.

"Thank you, Arnaud. Insightful as ever." She took out a handful of coins and dropped them into his palm. "A little extra too--"

"Ma'am!" A slender man with plaited, long brown hair ran towards them. He clutched a rifle in one hand and used the other to mop the sweat from his brow.

"Yes, Arthur?" Molly didn't like being interrupted, but she knew her men would only do it if necessary.

"There's..." He caught his breath. "There's some sort of battle."

"Yes? That's what we're all preparing for." Molly crossed arms.

"No! Outside, right now!"

"What?" Molly jumped to her feet.

"It's Crow and... I don't know. Some others, they're fighting, just outside the gates."

She strapped the pieces of brass to her knuckles. "Men! Prepare your weapons and follow me." She strode out of the main hall and down the corridor as fast as she could. Her leg had never fully healed, but she had enough men to make sure that wouldn't be an issue.

Pirates of Nassau

"Seem's Crow thought he could breach the walls. Ha! For as long as I'm still breathing, nobody ever shall! We will show them what we're made of! Why Thad owns Nassau." She let out a howl and the men joined in. "The call of the Coyote will haunt them, even in death!" She raised her fist as she marched down the hall. On her approach two men pulled thick chains and raised the door to the grounds. Molly stepped outside and into the palm-filled land which separated the house and the main gate.

"Arthur, have they stepped on any of the clams yet?" Molly asked.

"No, they're too busy fighting. Haven't even tried the main gate yet," Arthur replied.

"Keep the gate shut until I say otherwise." Molly stormed over to the ten-foot-high thick stone wall and climbed the ladder which ran to the top. Her eyes fixed on the guard who shook his head, his eyes filled with worry. "What is it?"

"They're dead ma'am, all of them," the guard said and looked away.

"What do you mean?" Molly peered over the edge.

"I watched... saw it all happen. Crow and his men were marching towards us, up the hill, and then they got ambushed by another group." He pointed down at the scattered bodies which lay across the grounds outside the wall. "A few went flying into the moat—"

"Ambushed? By whom?" Molly narrowed her gaze. She made out a couple of bodies with Vella's signature dreadlocked hair, some of Crow's motley crew too. "The fox, -- Jane Hatch's people." Molly pointed to a flag which lay on the ground next to a body. "They can't all be dead! I don't believe it. It's a trick."

"But there's blood ma'am, I saw them get shot." His hands shook as he stared at the floor. "I'm sorry ma'am, I should have--"

"Open the gate!" Molly glared at him as she clomped down the ladder. She winced with each rung as her wounded leg flared. Her foot touched the bottom, and she turned to her men. Around thirty stood waiting, ready for action with various blades and pistols in hand. "Shoot the idiot, Arthur. What sort of a guard doesn't alert me sooner."

Arthur nodded and raised his rifle. "Never liked him anyway."

Molly paused and waited for the snap of gunfire to settle. "Now, do you remember where you planted the clam bams?" she asked.

Pirates of Nassau

The men nodded in agreement. Several swayed with their eyes shut. They had been drinking solidly for days now but downed Molly's liquid courage at the last minute. The concoction supposedly absorbed any ill after effects from drinking. That way the men could have the drunken confidence to charge into battle and give it their all, but still remain sharp... though it didn't seem to be working. The main gate rattled open and Molly pushed any thoughts of her men's shortcomings to the back of her mind. She stormed through the gates arch, over the bridge and out into the field littered with bodies. Her eyes searched for any signs of movement. Nothing. Her men followed close behind. "Check they're dead. Take their weapons." The men staggered about the field poking and kicking at the bodies.

Her eyes scoured the area. She made a left and hurried past body after body with no sign of Crow. "Find anyone with a Captain's jacket and bring them to me!" she yelled. She narrowed her eyes. They stopped on a black-jacketed man with a blood-soaked long gray beard. "That fucker!" Molly stormed toward his body, blinded with rage. She towered over him. There was no sign of movement. "I was meant to kill you. An eye for an eye!" she said through gritted teeth. She clenched her fists and jaw in rage as she stared down at his face. It wasn't meant to be like this. She needed vengeance. For a moment everything around her disappeared into the darkness. She'd been dreaming of tearing Crow limb from limb, making him pay for snatching away her chance to change things with her son. But it was too late. She grabbed his jacket collar and went to lift him off the ground but a hot burning pain stopped her. The snap of gunfire rang through the air.

"You!" she yelled as she dropped to her knees. Her leg seared with pain. It was unbearable. She toppled to the ground and tried to drag herself away but to no avail.

"Surprise!" Crow rose up to sitting with a smoking flintlock pistol in hand.

Molly tried to reach out and grab him but for once she felt weak. Screams of agony filled the air. She looked around to see her men stumbling about and dropping to the ground. She was right. They had been tricked. Her breath quickened as pain surged through her body. How could she have been so stupid, so consumed by rage.

She lay on her front and turned her head to the side. She couldn't even crawl away. He'd shot her good leg and the other was too sore to propel her body away. "You bastard!" she said through labored breaths.

"You should have left things alone," Crow said and raised his pistol toward her head. "Bye Thad, or whatever your name is."

Isaac Carver

"No!" Isaac leapt in front of Crow, shielding Molly. "We don't have to do this."

"Get out the way, boy." Crow kept his pistol in place. "Don't you want the treasure? If we don't do this, there's no treasure!"

"Can't you just..." Isaac looked back at Molly who lay face down, blood poured from her leg. "Just, let her live? We'll be sailing away soon enough."

Crow waved his pistol and motioned for Isaac to move, but he stood firm. Crow glared at Isaac with a look of confusion. "You came up with this plan, the fake blood, the playing dead. If you didn't want her killed you shouldn't have done all this." Crow threw up his arms and swiped at the air.

Isaac rubbed his palms over his face. "I know, I know, but--"

"But nothing, move!" Crow yelled and pushed Isaac aside. "She won't stop hunting us down until we're dead."

Molly turned her head to the side and tried to push herself up. "He's right," she said through gritted teeth. "You killed my only son. I'll never stop until you're dead."

Crow shook his head. "First of all, I didn't know he was your son. I didn't even know you were...you!" Crow looked at Isaac. "She killed Nelson. Remember that boy, you were there. It was her orders." Crow shook his fist at Molly. "He didn't deserve that end."

Pirates of Nassau

Isaac shrugged. Crow was right... "Well, I tried." His shoulders sank as he looked back at Molly and frowned. "I'll miss our chess matches." He pressed his lips together and turned away. He'd picked his side, but he couldn't watch this. They'd been friends, of sorts anyway. They had something, a bond. At least he did with Molly but not Thad. Still, Molly had been lying to him for years. How could he ever trust her? His thoughts were angry but his heart filled with sadness at the thought of her being gunned down.

Crow took a step forward. "This is for Nelson," he said and raised his pistol.

Isaac tensed and held his breath.

Boom!

A series of explosions erupted. Crow stumbled backwards and lowered his gun. "Don't move," Isaac said and checked the surrounding field for whatever exploded. Joy ran toward them. "Isaac! Behind you! Run!"

"Don't listen, don't move! I think whatever is exploding is buried around us," Isaac's eyes searched for the source frantically.

"You would be right." Molly gave a wry smile.

"What are they Molly? Help us get out of here, and we can team up? It doesn't have to be like this," Isaac said as more explosions erupted.

Crow shot him a glare. "In your dreams, boy."

"We've got company." Molly motioned with her head behind them.

"Captain Crow! Don't move another muscle," an unfamiliar voice spoke. Isaac swung around to see nearly fifty men running out from the dense foliage surrounding the castle. They were led by a tall weathered man wearing a black and red captain's jacket. Isaac looked to Crow whose face said it all. Pistols were pointed at them from all angles and explosives surrounded them. There was nowhere left to turn.

Isaac patted at his inside pockets hoping for something to help them out of this mess. He felt the crinkled map and sharp edge of the cards but nothing more. "Do you know him?" Isaac asked.

Crow shook his head.

Pirates of Nassau

"Well, he seems to know you!" Isaac said. His heart sunk. Why did they get themselves into this?

"Put the pistol down, Crow. On the ground in front of you," the man in the captain's jacket ordered. This man stared at Isaac but every time he tried to catch his gaze he looked away. Something about him seemed odd yet familiar.

"You put yours down first," Crow said.

"The boy gets shot if you don't," the man said and pointed his pistol at Isaac.

Crow looked to Isaac and lowered his gun without hesitation. He crouched and placed his pistol on the ground in front of him. "We're out of luck boy."

Isaac searched the faces of the men before him. He didn't recognize any of them. They each wore a black bandana and vest with some sort of snake and skull painted on them.

"Who are you?" Crow asked and put his hands in the air. Isaac followed his lead.

"It's you!" Molly said with a tone of disgust. She tried to push herself up but couldn't.

"Indeed it is. I'm sure you thought you'd got away from us." The weathered man smiled and revealed a missing front tooth. "But I never got what was promised to me. I'm still missing half a map." The man took out a piece of torn tattered parchment and held it up.

Isaac's eyes grew wide. He tried to show no reaction but it proved difficult. There was the other half to their map.

"So where is it? You might as well tell us 'cause we're about to ransack your place and find it anyway," the weathered man said.

"It's not in there." Molly scoffed. She grasped at her leg and scowled in Crow's direction.

"Who the hell are you?" Crow asked again and shook his head.

"I'm The Boss, Captain Crow," the man said with confidence and turned his gaze to Isaac. He appeared thrown off guard and Isaac couldn't help but stare.

The Boss? What a stupid name Isaac thought. He eyed the man closely, those eyes were filled with a delirious hate. And again, they seemed familiar.

Pirates of Nassau

"Round them up, bind their wrists. We'll decide what to do with them in a moment. Get the girl too." He pointed in Joy's direction. Three men dragged her toward them. She kicked and screamed every inch of the way.

"Pff, didn't even hurt," one of the men said. He wiped a spot of blood from his leg. "Barely even a cut, love."

"Ha! You'll see," Joy yelled as they dragged her over and shoved her down next to Isaac.

Isaac knew Joy's tricks and that blade would most definitely be poisoned.

A man with a hook hand used a wooden club to hit Crow in the back of the legs. Crow dropped to his knees. Isaac saw Crow squint with pain, but he made no sound.

The man with the hook hand moved over to Isaac who knelt before he had a chance to hit him.

"Coward," the man with the hook hand said.

"Or clever," Isaac muttered under his breath.

A sweaty man shoved Joy to the ground. She knelt alongside Isaac and Crow.

"Get the beast too!" The Boss let out a short laugh. "You cost me a lot of business when you escaped. You'll pay for that."

Several of the black bandana-wearing men ran over to Molly and dragged her to be in line with the others. Molly did what she could to make it difficult, but she couldn't hide the pain in her face as they pummeled her and dragged her through the dirt.

The hook-handed man stood before Joy and waggled his crotch in her face. Joy spat at him. "Fuck you Leon!"

Isaac's chest tightened as Leon continued to harass Joy.

"That fire in you, I love it." Leon scraped the point of his hook down her face.

"Go any further and I'll bite your cock off!" Joy yelled.

The men all laughed.

"I'd like to see you try," Leon said and turned to the men.

"Ha! Is it too small? Is that what you're saying?" Joy smirked.

The men erupted in more laughter, elbowing one another and leering at Joy.

Pirates of Nassau

Isaac squirmed. Joy was full of fire; it was part of her appeal but it always got them into trouble.

"Shut up!" Leon smacked her across the face. His hook tore at her cheek.

Isaac winced. He hated to see her hurt.

"What do you want with us, Boss? Or should I call you Mr. Boss?" Crow said.

"You're in no position to mock me." The Boss smacked Crow across the face with his closed fist.

Crow shook it off. He puffed out his chest and stared at the weathered man. "If it's coin, we ain't got it."

The Boss swaggered up and down grinning. "A poor pirate? Not sure if I believe that one. We're not poor, are we boys?" He swung around and looked at his men who cheered in agreeance. "But then again, we're the one's holding the pistols. I think you've lost your touch Crow. I remember when you used to spend mountains of doubloons without a second thought."

Crow shifted from one knee to another and grumbled.

"I don't know what we want with you...yet. What do you think boys? Any ideas?" He turned to his men and flashed a wicked smile.

Isaac stared at the scene unfolding before him. The name clicked into place. This was the man Joy spoke of, The Boss. He was the one selling children to someone in Devil's Cay. He had Rose. Isaac swallowed the pressing lump in his throat.

"I've got some ideas for her," a toothless man stroked at Joy's face. Isaac could see the rage blazing in her eyes.

"Oh, just kill 'em already, I want to go in that place!" A tall hairy man pointed to Thad's castle.

"Sounds good!" The Boss agreed and laughed. "Though?" He tapped his forefinger on his chin.

"John!" Molly yelled out of nowhere.

"What?" The Boss said and scrunched up his face.

"You're John fucking Carver!" Molly shuffled a little and tried to steady herself to her feet but several men pushed her back down.

"John..." Isaac said under his breath. He couldn't believe his ears. He stared at the man's weathered face in disbelief. "My. Father?"

"I knew I recognized you. I've been around these parts longer than most," Molly said and held her chin up in the air. "You can only hide for so long." She smirked.

"I wasn't hiding! You're the one hiding! Hiding behind this!" The Boss waved his arms in the air. His face grew red, and he balled the fist of his pistol-free hand. "Nassau isn't yours anymore... you, you..." He stormed over to Molly and cracked his black wood pistol across her face. "We don't need your help. We'll find the rest of that map ourselves."

She shook it off and tried to headbutt his crotch but with no luck. "At least I wouldn't murder my own son!" Molly spat out a mouthful of blood onto his boots.

"Kill her! Now!" The Boss ordered and looked square at Isaac.

"Gladly," Leon said and picked up his wooden club.

"Beat her to death," the Boss said with such venom that Isaac even saw Crow wince.

"Don't ever trust him, Isaac!" Molly yelled as Leon and five others stormed toward her. Leon swung his club in a circle and smashed it down into Molly's leg. Isaac winced. Anybody else would have screamed in pain but not Molly.

"Not so tough now are you!" Leon shouted and smashed his club across her back. The others joined in, kicking at her sides and stomping on any part they could. Isaac watched in horror. He told himself to look away, but he couldn't. Leon screamed as he hit her across the face. They pummeled her over and over until her body lay still.

Isaac wanted to drown out the noise. His stomach knotted and churned. He looked over at Joy who stared down and didn't move. Crow kept his gaze straight ahead. These men were brutal, and led by his own fucking father. This monster was the man who left him with nothing. The abusive alcoholic he assumed dead. And now he was to die by his hand.

"Yes!" Leon tossed the blood coated club aside and raised his hook.

"Stop! She's dead!" Isaac yelled.

"Shut it!" Crow snapped through gritted teeth.

Leon turned to Crow, his face splattered with blood. "And you're next old man."

Pirates of Nassau

Isaac's vision grew cloudy. His heart thumped in his chest. He shut his eyes. The lump in his throat throbbed. Isaac sensed a presence close. He opened his eyes to see his father standing before him.

"It's just business son. She would have done the same."

Isaac looked over at Molly. Blood poured from her head and seeped into the ground. Business or not, no one deserved that kind of end, he thought. He looked into his fathers eye's. It had been so long since he'd seen him, but that cold stony hate still shone through. "What next? You kill Crow? Then me? Your own son! It wasn't enough you left me to die once with nothing, now it has to be by your hand!" Isaac choked back tears. He didn't want to cry, he didn't want this man to witness the hurt in his heart. He thought of that moment. The moment he played over and over in his head. He'd tried to drink it away. To blot it out. His father locked him in that coop with nothing. To starve to death. To die. And now this. The hurt vanished and the anger took over. Isaac stared into the eyes of this monster.

His father crouched before him. "I wouldn't kill you boy, I was just waiting for Thad to be out of the way. Now, that's taken care of, what say you join us? We can try be a family again? Can't we?" He smiled but his eyes didn't crinkle. "I've changed."

Isaac could feel the tears welling. He wanted so desperately to believe him. "Then why didn't you come back for me?"

John shrugged. "I was a drunk. I didn't think you were alive. I'm better now, haven't touched a drop in years."

Isaac shook his head and stared at the ground. There was no way he didn't know he was alive. Everyone in Nassau knew him. This prick was lying, just like he always did. He hadn't changed.

"Untie him." John beckoned to the tall hairy man who sauntered over and cut the rope on Isaac's wrists.

"Now can we go, Boss?" the hairy man asked and pointed to the castle.

"Of course, come Isaac." John held out his hand to Isaac. "Finish off the rest." He waved his hand in Joy and Crow's direction. "Then we raid that place!" He pointed to the thick stone walled castle and walked towards it.

Isaac scrambled to his feet. He couldn't feel his legs. He looked over to Crow who nodded and smiled.

"Don't worry about me boy." Crow returned his gaze to staring straight ahead. He puffed out his chest and held his head high.

He couldn't even bear to look at Joy. He had to save them or try at the very least.

"Crow first but then make sure you leave the beautiful Joy for me," Leon said and snatched up his blood-soaked club.

"Get the treasure, boy, for me and for Nelson!" Crow shouted as Leon raised his club.

Without wasting another second Isaac hurled himself between Leon and Crow. He lost balance and the three tumbled to the ground. "The treasure! I have the map!" Isaac yelled and grabbed Crow by the arm. The pair scrambled to their feet.

"You fucker!" Leon reached out and grabbed Isaac by the leg, but he kicked his hand away.

Click.

At least twenty barrels now pointed at them. "Don't shoot! I have the other half of the map! Molly wasn't lying, she didn't have it. I do," Isaac yelled and put his hands above his head. His heart raced. His father stopped in his tracks and turned to face him.

"I should have known you'd try something." John folded his arms. "No son of mine wouldn't." He gave a wicked smile.

"Let them go and you can have it," Isaac said.

"How about I have it and don't. Besides, what says you're not lying to me?" John said.

"Why kill them? Thad's gone. They won't cause you any trouble. You have Nassau. And you have my word."

"A notorious Captain and a bounty hunter? I'm sure they won't," John curled his lip in disdain. "You think I'm stupid?"

"No, what would that make me? Father." Isaac tried to evoke some sort of emotion other than hate.

"Show it to me, the map," John said.

Isaac reached into his pocket. His hand brushed his flask which sparked an idea. He grabbed out the pewter vessel and searched for the map. His hand struck the folded tattered parchment. He took it out and waved it in the air. "See?"

Leon reached for it but Isaac snatched it away. John's eyes grew wide. Isaac remembered that look. That insatiable greed.

"Let them go and the location of Kidd's thirty thousand doubloons is yours." Isaac nodded. The eyes of every man around him lit up. "What do you say, father?"

"There's not much stopping me from just taking that map and finishing the lot of you off," John said.

"Just shoot him!" Leon said.

"I'll make that call!" John shouted. "He's my son and I'm the boss. Don't you forget it!"

Isaac recognized that face. His father was about to unleash his rage. Isaac took the flask and unscrewed the lid. "Might as well." He took a sip and swished the contents in his mouth.

"I'm sick of this! He's only important when it suits. Just shoot the fucker!" Leon yelled.

John stormed over to Leon and grabbed him by the throat. Isaac seized the opportunity to shred the map. He quickly tore at it and scrunched it up into pieces then stuffed them into his mouth and chewed. He wanted to gag. The foul dry texture soaked up any moisture from his mouth. He took another sip of the rum.

"Boss!" the tall hairy man shouted.

"What?" John yelled. He held Leon in his grasp and snapped his head to see. "What in the?" He dropped Leon.

Isaac stuffed another piece in and chewed. Then spat the gnawed contents on the ground. He coughed and spluttered. John grabbed him by the scruff of the neck and shook his body to and fro. John's chest heaved with rage. His face turned red. A pistol barrel pressed into Isaac's stomach.

"Now I'm the only one who knows the location so you better listen to me," Isaac said.

"I should kill you now." His fathers gaze didn't falter. He looked him hard in the eye and pressed the barrel deeper.

"But you want that treasure," Isaac said. He knew it was a risk, but he was out of options. He hoped somewhere deep down inside his own father couldn't actually kill him. "Take me with you but let them go."

John released his grip and took a long deep breath in. He swung around and looked at the faces of his men. A few sprinted off in the direction of the castle. They clearly couldn't wait anymore.

"Let's torture him, he'll speak up then," Leon said.

"I'll speak anyway, you just have to let them live. Why are you so intent on killing everyone?" Isaac yelled.

John paced, his eyes looked to be searching for answers. Isaac didn't want to give him too much time.

"You have my word. I'll join your crew, lead you to the treasure but you have to let them live." Isaac waved his hand to where Joy and Crow knelt. "They'll write books about you y'know." Isaac looked at Joy's beautiful soft face. Blood trickled down her cheek. She stared at John with hard unfaltering eyes. He looked to Crow. He'd kept his chest and head held high this whole time. A wry smile spread across his face. Death didn't frighten him. He was a brave man and more of a father to him than this prick ever would be. It was then he realized that, for the first time in his life, he cared about someone other than himself. These people were his friends, his family even, and he knew that to save them he would sacrifice the world. His world. "Father, what do you say?"

John walked towards Isaac. "My son, a Serpent of Death, who'd have thought."

Leon threw down his club and spat.

John looked up and down. "You'll join my crew alright but you'll never so much as even look in their direction again. They're dead as far as you're concerned! Hear me?"

Isaac nodded.

"You can't possibly believe him!" Leon shouted and shot John a glare.

"He'll help us find it Leon. You mark my words, because if he doesn't, I'll hunt each of them down and strangle them to death myself." He pointed to Crow then Joy and turned to Isaac.

Pirates of Nassau

He grinned. Something in that smile unnerved Isaac, but he had no choice. "Now lead the pillage of Thad's place and reserve the finest cell on the ship for this one." John pushed Isaac toward Leon.

"What?" Isaac said as two men grabbed his arms. "But I thought..."

"Thought what? You'd be roaming the ship free? You might be my son but I'm no idiot," John said and scowled at Isaac. "I'll keep up my end of the bargain for now, but you'll need to earn my trust."

Isaac's insides wrenched. "Still the bastard you always were," he uttered under his breath.

"We set sail tomorrow." John rubbed his hands. "Cut them loose." He waved in the direction of Crow and Joy. "Now, run! Before I change my mind."

Crow and Joy scrambled to their feet and glanced in Isaac's direction.

"I said run! And don't cause me any trouble again!" He prodded Molly's broken limp body with his foot. "I got what I wanted."

Isaac's feet dragged in the mud as two men pulled him away, and he watched his friends sprint off into the distance for the last time.

Joy Lafitte

Joy took a sip from her rum-filled cup. Her eyes fixed on an intricate naval painting and moved across to the navy drapes which sheltered them from the searing sun. Vella's house didn't quite match what Joy knew of Vella but then again, she hoped her house didn't match what people knew of her, just for very different reasons.

"So that's it? He's part of their crew now?" Popino asked and interrupted Joy's daydream. Her heart filled with sadness at the memory of Isaac being dragged away.

"They'll be going to Devil's Cay so hopefully we can rescue him there," Joy said and nodded as if trying to convince herself.

"We'll get him back," Slim said and kept his head down. He didn't move his eyes from the map as he busied himself plotting points. "Get me brother too."

Georgia poked her head around the door. "How's the patient?" she smiled at Popino.

"Getting there," Popino said and returned the smile though it didn't seem sincere. He had moved from a makeshift bed to an armchair. Joy noticed the way Georgia eyed him. She could tell her behavior made Popino feel uncomfortable and that amused her since he was usually so obsessed with women. Georgia shot Popino a wink and disappeared.

Pirates of Nassau

"I can't believe that man is Isaac's father. I don't even remember what he looks like. Did they mention Rose?" Popino wrung his hands together.

Joy shook her head. "Maybe Isaac will find her before we do." She forced a smile.

"Let's hope." Popino nodded. He shut his eyes and let out a sigh. "And where's Crow?"

"Gone to check on the ship," Joy said.

"Black Beauty. She's a delight. You wait until you see her." Slim stared off wistfully into the distance.

"I think I did." Joy put her cup aside and took off her hat. "It's not in great shape but those doubloons should help with that." She walked over to a polished copper pot which sat on a shelf. She had avoided checking her reflection up until now. The gash on her cheek still stung and though she'd cleaned it up, it wasn't pretty.

"It will fade," Popino said.

Joy swung around and shrugged. She strode over to the seat next to Popino and sat down. She hated that she had a permanent reminder of Leon across her face. She bit her lip and tapped on her cup of rum.

"You know what there is in Devil's Cay, Miss Joy?" Slim said and rubbed his hands together.

Popino shook his head and leaned across to Joy. He spoke under his breath. "Do we really need him?"

"Melons!" Slim said.

Joy let out a huge hearty laugh for the first time in a long time. Slim was odd but he certainly lightened the mood. "You love those melons don't you Slim?"

"Oh, Miss Joy, I long for another taste of that juicy fruit!" Slim licked his lips.

"Soon enough," Joy said. She welcomed the distraction.

Popino rolled his eyes. "Again with the melon talk!"

"You're just jealous," Slim replied and jigged in his seat.

Out of nowhere, the door slammed open. Joy instinctively grabbed her blade, jumped to her feet and tensed, ready for action, only to see Crow standing there with his fists clenched.

Pirates of Nassau

"I can't." Crow stomped his way into the room. He switched between punching the air and rubbing at his head with his hands.

"Can't what?" Joy poured him a cup of rum and thrust it into his hand. He looked down and shook his head. "Whatever it is, this will make you feel better," Joy said.

Crow took a gulp and wiped at his mouth with the back of his hand.

"Is it... Isaac?" His name escaped her mouth, and instantly she wanted to take it back. She didn't want to hear what might have happened to him.

Crow shook his head. His eyes looked red as if he'd been sobbing.

"It's not the boy." Crow gulped the remainder of the rum down. "Top her up. I can't..." He shook his head.

"Just tell us!" Popino shouted. "Sorry, I just can't take much more. I don't think any of us can."

"It's Black Beauty. She's gone." Crow stared ahead dead-eyed.

"Gone? Stolen?" Joy asked.

"Burnt to a crisp. Woodman Jack too," Crow replied.

Joy's eyes grew wide. She looked at Popino whose mouth fell open.

"I liked Jack," Slim said. The corners of his mouth turned down.

"He was a creep, but he didn't deserve that. I'm guessing we know who's responsible?" Joy said. Her hands shook as she tried to remain calm. She was so close. They were so close. She swallowed the mounting lump in her throat. Crow handed her a piece of paper and took off his hat. She fumbled to open the note. Inside was a rough sketch of a human skull with three snakes slithering in and out of the eye holes and mouth. She read the words written underneath aloud, "Serpents of Death." She tossed the paper onto the nearby table. "Fuck them! I swear I'll hunt down those... those--"

Crow covered his face with his hat and screamed. Joy raised her brows and looked to the floor as the captain screamed again. He took away his hat and swiped the bottle of rum then tipped the contents into his mouth and slumped down against the wall.

The room fell silent.

"Those bastards." Slim sat back in his chair and folded his arms.

Pirates of Nassau

Joy paced back and forth across the room trying to muster a clear thought but nothing came to mind other than fury. She looked to Crow who sat with his head between his knees, defeated.

"What are we going to do without a ship?" Popino put his hand to his chest.

Crow shook his head. His eyes looked glassy. "We're fucked!" he shouted.

Joy puffed out her cheeks and let the air escape slowly. She hadn't ever heard the Captain sound so defeated. She plonked herself down in the chair next to Popino and put her head in her hands.

"I've got an idea," Slim said and pushed the map aside.

"Please don't let it involve melons," Popino half joked.

Joy looked up. "What is it Slim, go on." She looked him in the eye and nodded in encouragement.

"You've got that coin Miss Joy, the one from Jane." Slim sat forward and looked around as if checking for people listening. "We could borrow a ship with it." He sat back, his eyes shone with mischief. "How about The Fancy?"

Joy's brows dipped to a frown. "Jane's dead though. That coin's only good if people can call in a favor from her." Joy took out the small silver coin and placed the button-sized piece in her palm. She stared down and wondered what Jane would do.

"Why The Fancy? It's huge. Couldn't we get something that needs a smaller crew?" Popino said.

"It's Jane's ship." Slim crossed his arms and smiled.

Joy raised her brows in surprise. The rumor was, The Fancy belonged to the governor. How had Jane come to acquire such a ship, she wondered. "I can't believe it's her ship," she said under her breath.

Slim nodded.

Joy shook off the surprise. "But they'll know, her people will know?" she said.

"Word won't have spread yet." Slim shook his head. "It will just be a rumor. She's just missing for now. We ask for one week, but then we steal it!" Slim pointed his bony finger into the air and grinned.

Joy's mouth fell open, stunned. "That's--"

Pirates of Nassau

"Genius!" Crow scrambled to his feet. "I don't know what this coin is but looks like we're going to Devil's Cay." He walked over and slapped Slim on the back.

"You think it will work Slim?" Joy walked over to him.

"Oh yes Miss Joy," Slim replied and grabbed the map. "I've plotted the route there but it won't be an easy ride." He rolled up the parchment and clutched the scroll in his hand. "There will be foul sea beasts like nothing you've ever seen before. Waves so high they could engulf all of Nassau, but don't let that scare you." He grinned.

"Okay," Popino nodded, his face looked doubtful.

"I'm not scared. I'm sick of this life on land anyway." Crow gave Slim a nudge. "Right, I've got a crew to assemble!" Crow smacked his hands together and gave them a rub. "You'll be the second best crew I've ever had!"

Popino scrunched up his face. "Thanks?"

"We're back!" Crow slapped Slim across the back and laughed. Slim rocked forward with the force. "Meet me down at The Fancy in fours hours, we'll leave right away!"

Joy took in a deep breath as she walked down the dock towards The Fancy. She'd never sailed before but the idea sparked a fire inside her. Though her heart pinched at the thought of leaving Raven for so long, at least Tom and Jim would keep a close eye on her. She reassured herself as she leapt over a hole in the timber jetty.

As she drew closer she marveled at the magnificence of the vessel they were about to acquire. She squeezed the coin in her palm and jogged down the dock only to find Crow and Popino already loading up the ship.

"What's going on? How are you--"

"Nice of you to join us," Popino said. He clutched at his side with one hand and pushed items over to Crow with the other.

Crow turned to face Joy. "It's ours! Well, for now." He winked. "I told Richard you've that coin. He just needs to see it." Crow motioned to where a short balding man stood holding his hat with both hands looking rather shaken.

Pirates of Nassau

"I told Richard you've the coin. I know him from working down here," Popino said.

Crow rolled his eyes and mocked Popino.

Joy shook her head at the pair and walked over to Richard.

"Miss Joy I assume?" the balding man asked in a soft voice, his gaze fixed on the ground.

"Indeed I am." She smiled and tried to catch his eye which seemed to put him at ease.

"Please tell me you have the coin?" He looked around. "Popino told me you did but that man—"

"Of course!" Joy held out the silver in her outstretched palm.

"Sorry, just that man, he's erm quite forceful. Threatened me then just started loading stuff on but Popino said you'd make it right. I know him from working down here, on the docks." Richard scratched at his arm.

Joy nodded.

"I've looked after her, the ship for some time for Miss Hatch but never had the chance to speak with her." He looked to the floor. "I could use that favor -- we, my family could," Richard said.

Joy's heart sank. She wanted to ask why, or what he needed but by the same token she didn't want to know. She reminded herself the reason she was doing this -- for Raven, for Rose, for all those other children and now for Isaac too. She looked into Richard's eyes, all filled with hope at the prospect of having his moment with Jane. "Hang on." She reached into her jacket and pulled out another coin, then took Richard's hand and pressed them both into it.

He opened up his hand and stared down. "What's this for?"

"For your troubles. Letting us borrow the ship. Putting up with him." She motioned with her head to Crow.

"Oh, it's really no problem, this is too much. My time with Miss Hatch is all I need." He held out the glinting golden doubloon to Joy.

Joy put her hands up. "I insist, I'm not taking this one back."

"Well, if you say so Miss. thank you." He bowed his head in respect.

Pirates of Nassau

Joy forced a smile and turned on her heel. She felt bad but hopefully that would soften the blow. Killing bad people for coin was one thing but stealing from regular townsfolk just didn't sit right.

Crow waved for Joy to hurry. "We're all ready!" In what short time she'd known him, she had never seen him so full of life.

"That didn't feel good," Joy said as Crow held out his hand to help her aboard. "Pff! Please." She swiped his hand away and rolled her eyes.

"Worth a try," Crow replied and stroked at his beard. "This way." He walked towards the stern of the ship where the wheel sat. Joy followed closely, she recognized some of the crew. They scaled the nets and wound in ropes ready to set sail. A few gave her a nod, a few leered. "Down here." Crow ducked and headed through a door. He turned to her, "Captain's Quarters." She could tell he was proud. Joy followed him into a grand room. She hadn't expected anything like this onboard a ship. In front of her sat a table that could easily seat ten people. Around it she recognized familiar faces -- Popino, Slim and...

"Grimm?" she cocked her head to the side.

"Miss Lafitte." Grimm raised his glass and gave her a nod. "You can have a seat next to me if you like?"

"You're no pirate!" Joy said.

"And neither are you." Grimm smiled and tapped the seat next to him. "Drink?"

"Sure." Joy took a seat opposite Grimm and looked around at several new faces.

Grimm poured two glasses of wine and handed one to Joy and one to Crow. "We start with the good stuff, save that god awful grog for when we no longer care."

Crow stood at the head of the table. "I'll make the introductions for our new crew." He nodded toward Joy then Popino.

Joy sat back in her seat and sipped at the fruity liquid.

Crow raised his glass. "We have Slim, our Sailingmaster. He knows these waters like no other and is a keen shot too." He spoke with such vigor that the liquid spilled from the cup with each sentence. "Next we have Grimm, our Master Gunner. We're a little light on weapons but you'll make good with what we've got." Crow took a sip of his drink.

Pirates of Nassau

"Don't play cards with him either. You'll always lose." Crow laughed and spluttered a little as some of the liquid went down the wrong way.

The corners of Joy's mouth turned down and her brows dipped to a frown. "Master Gunner?" she mouthed then raised one of her lowered brows in Grimm's direction.

"It's been a while since we've had Grieves to run the ship. If the rum runs out, we'll be looking to him." Crow grinned.

Joy stared at the broad-shouldered man sitting opposite her. His arms were the size of two thighs. Only someone of Molly's stature compared. Joy felt a twinge of sadness at the thought of her. She hadn't deserved that ending.

Grieves gave Crow a nod and topped up his glass which his massive hand dwarfed. At the far end of the table, a woman with pale green eyes and long black hair sat with her hands clasped in her lap. Joy marveled at her posture. She held herself with an air of calm, yet Joy could see a fire in her eyes. Next to her sat a slight man wearing a bright blue hat. He surely wasn't a pirate. Neither of these two were, Joy thought, though they were probably thinking the same of her. The blue-hatted man put down the sketchbook he was holding and looked straight at Joy. His gaze was piercing. She wasn't sure where to look.

"Right, who's next..." Crow looked around. "Arnaud! This one won't be getting his hands dirty, he's our thinker. Our spy. Them clothes are too nice to mess up anyway."

"They certainly are," Arnaud said. He stood, tipped his bright blue hat, crossed his legs and sat back. He still hadn't taken his gaze off Joy though she was used to this sort of attention and judging by the size of him she was sure he wouldn't cause her any trouble.

Crow walked over the woman with long black hair and placed his hand on her shoulder. She didn't move. "Fiona, the first woman to ever become part of my crew. I took some flack for that one but I'm glad I did." Crow patted at her shoulder. Fiona didn't make any expression. She kept a steely gaze. Crow scrunched up his face. "Where's?--"

"Under the table," Fiona replied.

Crow lifted the table cloth and motioned for who or whatever it was to come out.

A small woman crawled out and sprang to her feet.

Pirates of Nassau

"I know you!" Joy said. She hadn't meant to speak aloud but the surprise forced the words out.

"Nipper's like you with them blades." He nodded at Joy. "Our very own surgeon too. Hopefully that won't be needed though," Crow said and scratched at his beard. He looked to an empty seat next to him. His eyes glazed over as he reached into his pocket and retrieved a burgundy bandana. He gave it a shake and placed it on the chair then took off his hat and bowed his head. "Finally, let us raise a glass to Nelson. Gone but not forgotten." Crow rushed the words. Joy could tell he was struggling to keep it together.

"He'll always be with us. He would've loved to get a taste of melon," Slim said.

Crow nodded. "He would."

Grieves cocked his head to the side.

"It's a big fruit," Joy said.

"Miss Joy tried some didn't you," Slim said.

Joy's cheeks flushed with embarrassment at the attention. She usually brimmed with confidence but for once she felt surrounded by people that might well be more skilled than her.

"Ah the beautiful Miss Joy, we welcome you. I'm sure you'll fit right in. Can kill a man in a heartbeat, so I wouldn't try anything." Crow raised his glass in her direction and took a sip.

Popino coughed. "Leaving the best till last?"

Joy rolled her eyes at Popino's confidence, though it did bring a smile to her face, as did Crow's introduction. She wasn't usually proud of what she did for a living.

"Oh, I haven't forgotten about you," Crow said and took a gulp of his wine. "I spent a lot of years hating you but luckily that friend of yours set things right."

Popino shifted in his seat.

"This one's a good thief, though I'm assured those ways have changed. Good at getting hurt too." Crow gave a chuckle.

"And handsome," Arnaud added.

"I'll say," Fiona said. She kept her icy gaze but this time focused it on Popino. "Where's the friend?"

Pirates of Nassau

"Devil's Cay, my daughter too." Joy could see the light fade from Popino at the very mention.

"We'll get him back, the girl too. We wouldn't be on this ship if it weren't for the boy. Let's drink to him too. To Isaac!" Crow raised his glass and down the contents.

"To Isaac," Joy said softly. She hadn't expected to miss him half as much as she did.

"To Isaac indeed!" a voice came from the doorway.

Joy sat bolt up-right in her seat. It couldn't be? She turned around to see a rather disheveled Isaac practically jump through the door with flagons in each hand.

"Isaac!" Joy yelled. She couldn't get out of her seat quick enough.

Popino and Joy both ran over and threw their arms around him.

"I've never been so happy to see you. My god you stink." Popino turned away and scrunched up his face.

"You weren't going to leave without me now, were you?" Isaac laughed. He squeezed Joy tighter than he ever had. She let go and looked at his face.

"Did you see her?" Joy asked.

Popino's eyes grew wide. "Isaac?"

Isaac shook his head. "Rose is already on her way to Devil's Cay, they sent her on another ship, I'm sorry Pino," Isaac said.

Popino shut his eyes and nodded.

Joy returned to her seat. She needed to sit down. She couldn't believe he was here. She couldn't believe how she felt.

"Looks like Popino has competition," Fiona said under her breath and leaned into Arnaud.

Joy did her best not to react to the comment. It wasn't as if her and Isaac were even a thing anymore. She re-adjusted her jacket and tried not to seem ruffled.

"Grieves! I thought you died in the brothel?" Isaac said.

"Came close," Grieves replied. He had a much more jovial voice than what Joy had expected.

"Arnaud! I wouldn't have expected to see you here." Isaac grinned. "I'm sorry about Margaret."

Pirates of Nassau

Arnaud nodded and rubbed a gold locket which sat around his neck.

Joy looked to Crow who hadn't said anything. He shook his head and combed his hand through his beard.

"You not pleased to see me Crow?" Isaac joked.

Crow continued to shake his head. "How?" His eyes crinkled so much that they almost disappeared.

"Let's just say I used a trick I learned from a good friend." Isaac winked.

"Of course you did!" Crow grinned and strode over to Isaac. Joy could tell he was proud.

"He means me!" Popino said.

"I don't think so," Crow replied.

Isaac laughed. "You'd never believe it..." He pulled on his shirt which was a bit too tight for him. He sniffed at the air. "What's that?" His face dropped.

An older lady appeared. She walked with a stick and brought an air of musk and smoke with her.

"You!" Isaac said.

"Bonjour mon cher," the lady spoke with a husky French accent. She grabbed Isaac's arm and squeezed then brushed her body up close to him and shuffled past.

"You were right!" Isaac said.

"Of course." She coughed and hobbled over to a seat in the corner.

"Those cards, the crow, the dog missing a leg, the biting snake!" Isaac blurted his words out faster than Joy had ever heard him speak. "Why didn't you tell me more?"

"That wouldn't be any fun now would it." She shot Isaac a wink.

Crow laughed. "Pont Neuf is always right boy, and we never set sail without her. Glad you could make it at such short notice."

"I knew I'd be needed. I was ready." Pont Neuf caught her breath. Grieves rushed over to her with a drink. "Merci. We must cast off Captain."

"Right you are!" Crow rubbed his hands together and made for the door.

Pirates of Nassau

Joy looked to Isaac. Something in his eyes seemed different. There was a light in them that hadn't been there in all the years she had known him.

"Who's ready for an adventure?" Isaac grinned. "Before you go... Captain." Isaac reached for Crows arm and caught it. "Weren't we going to flip on that?" Isaac pulled out a silver coin and held it up to Crow.

"In your dreams!" Crow replied.

"But you're a man of your word." Isaac put his hand to his chest and feigned shock.

"Quartermaster?"

"Deal." Isaac smiled and followed Crow out. "I mean I don't know what one does but sure."

Want More?

Thank you so much for reading.

If you enjoyed this book please take a moment to write a short review. It will help other readers to find us and enjoy it too.

Also sign up to our mailing list to find out what we're working on next!

Join Us

Alternatively, you can find us all over social media Instagram @maplelionfiction Facebook @maplelionfiction Twitter @maplelionwrites

Wait there's more... you can drop us an email: maplelionfiction@gmail.com or visit our website https://www.maplelionfiction.com too!

Thank you again for reading.

We look forward to connecting with you soon :)

<<<>>>

Printed in Great Britain
by Amazon